Anna Apsley

Dedication:

This book is dedicated
to
Hermione and Simon

About The Author

Anna Apsley is a writer of fiction. She describes herself as 'a sea person' and all her adult life she has lived close to water and the sea. Anna loves playing with ideas and is interested in ecology and scientific theory.

Stilllwater is her letter to the future.

To know more about Anna please visit her blog www.annaapsley.wordpress.com

Contents page

Stillwater

The drop that you hold in your hand
is part of the water which was the cradle
of all life
on this planet aeons ago
the first rain that splashed down
on the hot earth
to form the first sea.
Each drop, in sunlight
has risen from the sea in countless ages
and fallen to the earth again
as rain

The drop that you hold in your hand
has been a prism forming myriad rainbows
has travelled underground streams
bubbling through dark caverns
the architect of cathedral caves
formed valleys
and split granite

The drop that you hold in your hand
has flowed down broad rivers
has risen in the sap of trees
has been the sweat of slaves
and the tears of children
it has become the foam topped waves
and deep unfathomable depths
of vast dark lakes and seas

The drop that you hold in your hand
has been part of the great flood
it has been a dewdrop on a blade of grass
a drop that has pounded through the
hearts of whales in blood
and lain in an eagle's egg
it has travelled in the fluid of a poet's brain
and dripped from the wounds of the dying

The drop that you hold in your hand
has been trapped in the snows of the arctic
reflected the sun in a desert oasis
and refreshed the weary

This drop unimaginably old
yet fresh and new
is evaporating slowly from your hand
to mingle with the air you breathe, perhaps
or drift in a sun-topped cloud
a thousand feet above the earth
imagine its journey from your hand
where will it go?
You can direct its journey
as it evaporates
send your consciousness with it
it is the water of Life
It is still water

This drop unimaginably old
yet fresh and new

The Darkness Comes

Viewed from space, the planet shone out like a dazzling sapphire spinning in the void. A vast sea covered the globe's surface. Its only solid features were an ice cap and a single splash of green — an Island set in a turgid sargasso sea, close to the equator. The Island, covered with abundant flora and fauna around its perimeter, was dominated by a great snow-capped mountain at its centre. From this high vantage point — in the pearl grey dawn — the great raft system could be seen many miles distant from the land.

* * *

Indra emerged from her raft hut into the brightening morning light. Closing her eyes she leaned against the eastern wall of her hut drinking in the warmth and newness of the day.

She sat down on the edge of the raft, dipping her hands into the sea and splashing her face with sparkling water. As she did so she gave thanks for the water that surrounded her. Her face suffused with inner light as she raised her arms towards the life giving rays, absorbing the new day.

After a few minutes she relaxed entirely — spreading out her mat and limbs — she lay down.

A slight breeze licked her body in its bath of warm sunlight. The waves slapping the logs beneath her made a pleasant rocking sensation as the silent white birds above her wheeled their giant air patterns into the blue void. She drank in these movements and began devising a feast dance in which others danced the sea movement whilst holding her spread-eagled and aloft.

How many women would it take to hold her up — maybe nine to hold her and more to dance the white birds wheeling above — as the waves of women lowered her to the deck. The drums would be gently rhythmic with the slate bells playing the music of sunlight.

Indra became aware that she was thirsty and sat up.

Immediately Mione came towards her smiling, carrying a small tray of steaming Papra leaves and honey. Putting the tray to one side for a moment she squatted down as they hugged each other in the cheek to cheek day greeting form.

'Greetings of morning Indra my mother. Shall I stay with you or do you wish to be alone while you drink your Papra?'

'Thank you Mione. I would like us to sit here together — but first would you get me a great dry leaf, my black paint and a writing brush from my box. I am creating a new dance for the feast time. Also I would like my shawls.'

Slowly she sipped from her small cup then rose and tied the shawls Mione had brought. The shawls were tied at either shoulder so that each fell from the neck across the breast to the opposite hip. The long shawl fringes brushed against her legs. The soft rainbow silk shawls were so beautiful to the touch that no-one who wore them could ignore their sensual quality. The raft women wore them almost every day as they moved about the rafts.

While Indra painted the stages of the dance Mione prepared more Papra and honey for them both. When she had finished they sipped the hot liquid whilst gazing out to sea. The Island was barely visible on the horizon.

'Do you know how many days will pass before we return to the Island Mione?'

'Leacia thinks we should begin to return in about seven days if the weather holds and the fish continue to fly. I am so looking forward to our return. It is my generation's time to learn to be gatherers and we will also help provision the male rafts as it is also their time of returning. I have never set foot on land before. Will you tell me about it again? I can't imagine what it is like not to be on the rafts.'

'The island moves just like our rafts — we can feel it in our bodies. Some the say it is our blood that moves and that the Island is still — I do not know the truth of it. But everything that has life has movement and I feel the Island's life movement. What is truth for us is truth for us — if you have been given your answer be content or live in the knowledge that several answers can hold parts of the truth. The sea is our home but the Island is our mother.'

'Oh Indra! I am so excited about going to the Island,' Mione's face was alight with passion. 'Next year will be the Choosing

Time at the feasts — my generation will be the centrepiece. I could be choosing my first! The males scare me a little, I'm glad we only see them once a year at the feastings. Where do they go? We never see them drifting around the Island like we do.'

Indra looked down into the beautiful depths of her young daughter's eyes. She felt a great surge of love.

'Mione, please get my brush from the hut. I will brush your hair. It is time to tell you what I know.'

Indra and Mione were unalike yet loved each other greatly. Indra was one of the most creative women on the raft system. She had an exquisite girl body and an expressive face that was not beautiful yet not plain. Light shone from her sparkling dark green eyes. In common with all raft women she had never cut her gold-brown hair. Mione had exceptionally large eyes, she was already taller than her mother with big hands and feet that meant she would probably become one of the taller raft people. She was a talented musician and dedicated to the practice of the most difficult stringed instrument of the raft people. She was also very intuitive to other peoples' needs, especially her mother's.

Indra took the brush and started the long rhythmic movements, savouring the scent of her daughter's body and the softness of her waist length hair streaked with gold. She also became aware of her own long hair caressing her back as she brushed.

'Our males go out much further than we do. They do not always stay in sight of each other. Sometimes the great sea storms out there part them. They do not sail for the shelter of the lagoons, they cannot sense storm from far off as we do. It is said they enjoy riding the storm's danger. I do believe it, my male child, Bjon was very adventurous and often came near to death due to his adventures. I handed him to the male raft at his life's third feast. I have not seen him since.'

'The males play games that are incomprehensibly boring to us. While they play many of them drink fermented drinks which sometimes make them fight each other. That is why they have to swim when they return to us at feast times. While they swim and cleanse themselves we 'clean' and search their rafts. We even swim under the rafts to make sure none is stored there. Our soft smoke at the feasting and dancing keeps them mildly sedated while they are with us and we have their usefulness and moon passion.'

Mione giggled a little, but she did not want to interrupt her mother's revelations. Indra smiled, and then grew serious.

'It is said they have a great raft at anchor where they store their fermented drink — somewhere out there beyond the horizon.

They also go beyond where the fish fly, searching for the land that is foretold. No males have ever found it or none have returned from it. Once it is found, it is foretold that the finding of it will begin the rolling of the stones and we will be forever changed.'

Mione shivered and turned to look into her mother's eyes.

'I don't believe it exists. Our Island is our sustenance and the fish that give themselves by flying onto our rafts and dying. How can the males do without flying fish if they go beyond these waters? I cannot imagine a day without the smell of cooking fish or do they smoke it and eat it dried?'

Indra stopped brushing her daughters hair. 'You are young to know these things but your questions must be answered to the best of my knowledge. You will not like the answer. Dalon, your brother's father told me this, so I will tell you. They put down nets to catch the ocean fish and bring them onto the rafts to die. I cannot imagine it. It is bad enough watching the flying fish dying on our rafts when they give themselves to us. I am always glad if one should fall back into the waves and swim away.'

'It's a horrible idea, Indra. How could they do it?' Drops of sea water ran down her cheeks.

'Do not cry Mione. I think perhaps we must believe as the men do that the fish choose to swim into their nets.'

'I am glad we do not do it'

'I agree,' replied Indra as she put down the brush and hugged her daughter. 'Enough of the males! Let us go and eat.'

Together they crossed the link bridge to the next raft which was still piled with water nuts. Beyond that raft was an agri-raft where sprouting beans were harvested. As they approached the more populated rafts Indra was glad that she lived on an outer raft not linked to any inhabited ones. She greatly enjoyed her self-imposed isolation. Mione's generation rafts were not too distant. At her age girls shared communal rafts together, later they could choose to share or not as they wished. As they crossed the great floating system women and girls approached them going in different directions along the walkways. Women called or waved in greeting as they saw each other from afar or if they met on the walkways there would be palm highs, hugs or just a nod in passing. Some women had young male children who would soon go to the male rafts, others had babes newborn.

Indra and Mione arrived at the eating raft and had a late breakfast. There were still some eggs left from the morning collection.

Flightless birds lived on the rafts and it was the morning delight of the children to run around collecting eggs from the birds ingenious hiding places. Each morning an egg collection would take place. The children would bring them to the eating raft in their small woven baskets. While their eggs were cooking on the hot stones they would scour the outer rafts to collect enough fish and eggs for everyone.

After breakfast some of the older girls would go to the water raft, collecting any flying fish that were not already harvested. They could never be gathered up until their life force had departed in case they chose to return to the sea with their last moments of struggle. Older girls would also make sure that the water catchers were still firmly anchored from the night. The water catchers resembled large inverted umbrellas made of waxed silk that caught the rain and dew into a funnel at the lowest point which drained into large containers. If the wind was too great they could be folded and furled with great speed. This water supplemented the supplies of Island water and stores of water nuts which held delicious thirst quenching juice.

When Indra and her daughter emerged from the sail shade of their breakfast table an eerie silence had fallen across the whole raft system.

All that could be heard was the whipping flap of slack sail, the choppy slap of wave against log and an uneasy tightening squeeze of wet rope.

Every visible woman had turned to face northwards. All were still. Along the rim of the northern horizon a thin black shadow lined with a strange red glow had ominously appeared. Everyone could sense a difference that was not storm change. It was drier than storm, felt highly charged, magnetic and dangerous.

Something extraordinary was happening out there — something unknown.

'Run for the Island!' The cry went up. Suddenly everyone began running to their rafts. Indra sprinted across the bridges they had crossed so slowly an hour before. Being an outer raft, hers must be one of the first to cast off. She knew that she must not hold the others up.

The moment she reached her raft she unhooked her link bridge from the nearest raft, unfurled her silk sail and tacked for the Island. Behind her the many other multi-coloured sails blossomed like fast growing flowers spreading out across the ocean., flowing away from the strange dark horizon.

Looking back Indra felt a deep disturbing fear.

Island

The sun began to set behind the mountain as the women gathered on the Island. The women's council sat crossed legged in a circle, facing outwards on the highest cliff above the shoreline. A hundred feet below them the raft city huddled in the bay. The women were dressed in their formal silks, their long hair gently breeze blown. All had painted mask-like faces, each voicing a wordless chant. Their commingled voices echoed the sound of wind in the star fields — a vocal essence that reached from earth to sky.

'We evolved from stardust and to the stars we will return.'

The answering worded chant floated up from the raft city.

Indra focussed her mind to travel northwards — searching. It was frightening, sending even a part of herself towards that dark mystery but that was the direction given as hers by the rune stones in the inner sanctum. She had had no alternative but to face her fear.

During the day the silk wing gliders had cruised around the Island, going far out to sea on the upward thermals. The darkness to the north remained and no male rafts had been sighted.

Within the circle the weirding descant reached its height. The women's voices filled the night air, searching — reaching out beyond the island — reaching out beyond the single star that glittered above them in the blood red sunset.

Suddenly, with an air of someone being called, Indra stood up and left the circle. With slow measured steps she walked towards the cliff edge. As she walked she undid the single knot of her light ceremonial robe under which she had tied her simple white tunic. Then cradling herself into the hammock harness under the skywing, she launched herself over the cliff. Gently floating in the tranquil air above the sunset colours she gave herself fully to the sensation of flight.

Indra felt strangely compelled to fly from the island nearer and nearer to the dark horizon. She had never flown so far from the Island. Her breathing became laboured. She felt burning prickling stabs of panic. A nauseating smell burnt into her nostrils. A fierce hot wind suddenly blinded her, sending her wing reeling backwards high into the atmosphere. She struggled with the violent chaotic movement of the wing. She felt unable to draw breath. The air became so cold she felt was turning to ice. She knew she was dying.

With a sense of detachment she watched herself finally drifting lower. Indra closed her eyes. A vivid picture of the configuration of the rune stones as they scattered around Her Eye flashed before her. They had shown that her path lay northwards. Had they also shown of her death? Suddenly able to breathe she drew a great shuddering breath. As her breathing stabilised she gradually realised that she was getting warmer.

Tentatively Indra opened her eyes. She saw the dark island surrounded by a sea of moonlit phosphorescence. Painfully she began to feel her blood flow again. Hope surged through her. Perhaps it was meant that she should return. Carefully re-adjusting her stiffened fingers grip on the wooden wing bar she turned towards the Island.

She had the sensation that she was in an air tunnel. The wing was drifting from side to side up the walls of the tunnel, but it kept her on course. She knew her strength was failing and that she lacked her usual control of the wing, control that she had learned as a child. Part of her mind was frightened by this lack of ability to steer the wing, although this concern seemed peripheral to a pervasive sense of well-being — a peacefulness that was profoundly moving, as she flew on helplessly through the moonlit sky.

Indra flew over the shadowed Island shoreline. Over the high rock and the smoking embers of the ritual circle. Strangely, it seemed to matter little that she was overshooting the usual landing points. She was being taken to the mysterious interior of the Island. Unable to change direction inside this invisible air tunnel she was being taken towards the great white sacred mountain, miles into the interior where no woman ever ventured. It was against all tradition and taboo that she should fly here. It was terrifying but also exciting. She was being taken inexorably towards the Island's great white heart.

Interior

The tall yeti woman emerged from the shadows of the cave. She had seen Indra's moonlight descent into mountain snow. Well over two meters in height, the woman had ankle length white hair which enhanced her beautifully angular face. Her eyes were exceptionally large and luminous in the silver starlight. Her skin, where exposed, was covered in a fine white down except for central features of her face and the palms of her hands. She looked a magnificent noble creature, framed in the moonlight against the dark cave mouth. The wailing wind blew through the high cold mountain passes as she strode towards Indra across the snowy wastes, automatically prodding the snow with her long white stick, like a thin third leg, as she walked.

Indra had fallen into a deep snow drift. An unerring second sense guided the yeti woman towards the limp warm body under the broken sky wing — a body that was getting colder.

In a few minutes tall woman had crossed the vast expanse of snow. She undid the harness and pulled Indra gently from the underwing hammock.

*   *   *

Indra awoke to the echoing sound of haunting reed pipes — a dry bitter-sweet music that spoke of the mystery and solitude of high places. It spoke of the majesty of starlight and of the great spirituality to which the human soul aspires.

When Indra opened her eyes her gaze rested immediately, and with some shock, on the largest being that she had ever seen. This creature had an ethereal quality and seemed to possess a radiant glow that bathed the cave in the warmth of her being. The yeti woman was by the fire. She was listening to the music with her eyes closed, tears coursing down her cheeks. There were lights around the cave, reflected in small water-filled plates. They threw softly undulating rainbow colours against the rock folded walls, making the cave a place of calm tranquility. The music ended on a low note that seemed to echo through the caverns for miles.

Indra found herself imagining that she was floating with that last long note, travelling into the heart of the mountain. The ending of the note drew attention to the silence beyond it. To a stillness that was enhanced by the note that had ceased, it was as if a vast wave of silence flowed back to engulf her. The woman smiled at Indra, a smile that was a gift and made Indra feel at peace in the presence of this giant.

'You are welcome to my home, raft woman.'

Indra had never heard such a deep resonant voice. It was a voice that seemed like many voices and yet one voice. It was as if an orchestra had spoken.

'Who are you' asked Indra, sitting up rather painfully. She felt as if she was a small child again.

'We are the Mountain Woman, Aaron. We live in this high place alone so that we may meditate on our star essence. Every being, Every creature, every rock, every droplet of water — earth herself is made of the elements of stars.'

27

A moment later she smiled.

'Indra, Indra, you look so serious. Be at peace. No harm will come to you. It was the star's light that brought you here.'

'Where am I? I was flying the wing towards the strange darkness. The wind lifted me far out of my way towards the mountain. But then... But then... I do not remember. I must return to the rafts. It is forbidden for me to be so far from the sea. I am compelled to return. You must let me go.'

Aaron walked over to Indra smiling and sat down before her with a noble grace and agility.

'Were you in control of your wing when you came to this place, Indra?'

'No. I could not control it. I felt as if I was wrestling with both wing and wind. First I was blinded by air that was burning. I could not breathe. Then I became frozen with cold. I overshot the landing places — I could do nothing.'

Taking Indra's small hand in hers Aaron said: 'You have been brought to me.'

'We have been expecting you, Indra. Do not be afraid. You are in need of rest and healing after your fall. You must stay here with me a while. You are the Island's special child and we must teach you certain truths about your people in order that you may fulfil your destiny. You are seeking the answer to the dark shadow beyond the northern horizon. The Rune stones were cast. You were chosen to search there. Be at peace, later you will know the reason for the commandment that calls you back to the sea.'

'How do you know my name?'

'We have known you from your first landfall. When as a young girl you first visited the Island to collect provisions with your generation.

'There is a passageway from here which leads to the roof of the Sacred Cave.'

'Watching from that place high in the cave we have watched over you and your people. One day the rock on which this Island sits will become part of the highest mountain ranges. From there, when the land is no longer the province of womenkind we will send our power of light through those shadowed ages.'

The yeti woman brought Indra an earthenware cup of warm herb tea.

'Drink this and sleep now, Indra. You need much rest'

Aaron sat beside Indra and cradled her head in her lap.

'It is warm here, you are safe. We will talk again after you have rested.'

Indra felt deliciously warm in the layers of multicoloured silk that was wrapped around her. She felt completely at peace. The beautiful yeti woman rhythmically stroked her forehead, humming softly. Soon, in the heart of the mountain, Indra fell into a deep sleep.

Noah's Children

During the days that she spent in the cave healing from her fall into the biting cold snow, Indra grew to love the giant woman who seemed to know her every need. She learnt that the mountain woman had used the term 'we' in a dynastic sense. There were no others present, only a succession of beings, each of whose lifetimes spanned hundreds of years. Each successive yeti woman had given birth to a daughter. Each daughter was instructed in the accumulation of thousands of years of knowledge passed down through countless ages.

Indra was fascinated by the beauty of the graceful movement that was totally natural and yet completely unexpected in the everyday actions of one so large. Aaron was a wonderful dancer. On many evenings Indra watched as the music stone was set by the fire to activate its store of ancient haunting music. Aaron, lithe as a panther, would sometimes leap breathtakingly high into the air. Yet at other times bringing a tear to the eye with the gentlest of emotional interpretations of the music. Indra sometimes thought it sad that these wonderful dances were never to be seen by others. When she expressed this thought Aaron answered that she danced in the flow of Spirit and that for all who truly dance, the dance itself is within them and needs no further perfection than the moment itself.

As she began to recover from her sky fall, Indra too began to dance — tentatively at first. It was exhilarating and she surprised herself at the new heights of performance she reached after only a short while. Dancing with Aaron was stimulating both physically and spiritually, and she knew she had begun to reach a new level of understanding of the dance within.

The voice of the mountain woman was strange to Indra's ears and, although she loved the slight soft accent of her friend's spoken word, she never felt entirely comfortable when Aaron sang. Aaron's voice was that of many voices that spoke as one. When she sang it was as if an otherworldly choir skimmed the stars.

One evening, when Aaron and Indra were sitting by the fire listening to music, Indra asked Aaron to tell her of the strange phenomenon that brought forth music from the stone. Aaron smiled.

'The stone is made of space and stardust — in everything there is more space than stardust. When warmed, the spaces in the stone get larger and the musical vibrations retained within the stone can be heard. You have become attuned to these vibrations while you rested here.'

Indra stared into the flickering firelight. A question had been burning within her for some time.

'Aaron, tell me about the island. You have told me that you and your ancestors have watched over us. Can you tell me what you know of my people?'

'From the pictures in the Sacred Cave you know some of the story, Indra. But you are right, there is much more that I can tell you.'

'Some of the pictures in our Sacred Cave by the shore are very like the ones here in the Hall of Echoes, Aaron.'

'Yes, we have been there but the other pictures are from the paintings of your ancestors, both male and female.'

Indra gasped. 'That can't be true. The males cannot come to the Island. It is forbidden.'

'It was not always so.'

Aaron poked the fire with a stick. Indra stared at the sparks that flew up into the dark folds of rock that formed the chimney. She thought about the pictures she had seen within the sacred cave and could see, with hindsight, that this could be true. The pictures that were thought to be the earliest were so very different in content and execution, that it was indeed an answer if they had been painted by the males.

'Yes,' said Indra, reflectively. 'I see it now.'

'Both males and females once lived upon this island,' continued Aaron.

Again Indra was in a state of shock.

'We lived on the Island?'

'Yes. Your ancestors were an island people, you lived together with the males in one village.'

Indra glanced up from the fire. 'I have much to learn.'

'Yes,' replied Aaron. 'There is much that you must know at this time of great change. Shall we continue or do you want to rest.'

'I want to know more, Aaron. I will not be able to rest until you have told me the whole of it. I thought that we had always lived as we do now. Surely we always had rafts?'

'In those days rafts were only taken out when your people gathered flying fish. The first big disagreement between your people was when the males wanted to make nets to try to catch the fish instead of waiting for their sacrifice. But the women's council forbade it. Unknown to the women, the males made nets which they kept on the other side of the Island. That was the first parting of your people. '

'The males would go off for days to the other side of the Island and use their nets. The women stayed in the village. The next disagreement began when the males decided they would seek the Great Spirit of the Stars, on the summit of the mountain. Several males died in the snows up here attempting to climb to reach the summit of Arrat. To seek the Way of the Spirit became an obsession. They began killing animals…'

Indra sucked in her breath sharply, in horror.

'…For fur to cover themselves against the cold. The silkworm population was seriously depleted as more and more silk was required for extra layers of clothing, rope, and rope ladders. When the women saw the males wearing the skins of animals the council of women was outraged. They felt they were no longer able to live with the males.'

'After the males departed, the women danced rituals to appease the spirits of the animals which had been killed. No weapons were allowed in what had, by now, become the women's village. But to the great sadness of the women the animals on the Island had become frightened of humans.

Birds no longer fed from their hands, animals ran from them. Even the children could no longer play with the Island animals because the animals now feared all humans. For a time it was an almost unbearable loss, but the women always welcomed the males back and tried to understand their reasons for doing these things. Even when they heard that the males were hunting and eating animals, they put it down to "male madness" and forgave them. It was rumoured that some men had heard the voice of Great Spirit.

They said that She had been calling them and urging them to continue their quest to reach higher.

'Still no male reached the summit of Arrat although the expeditions were getting a little nearer. Then someone thought of building a tower on the lower slopes, a vast tower that would be as high as the mountain so they could look across to the summit and see the home of Great Spirit. If the Great Spirit was not to be found there, they would build higher, to the moon and the stars.

This monumental idea was a complete disaster for the Island. The males chopped down tree after tree, year after year, until the tower was vast but the Island was dying. The people began to starve and many died. Winds buffeted the Island as never before and much of the Island became barren. The Island was dying. People were beginning to go hungry.

'Finally, my ancestor, Sumi, called everyone to the Sacred Cave. She had never shown herself to them before. The people were very much frightened by the appearance of a great white being with large silver cymbals, whose crashing sound reverberated around the Island. You have seen those great silver disks hanging at the entrance to the Sacred Cave.

Sumi was angry and told your ancestors that if they were to continue to live they must disassemble the tower and make more rafts from the wood. Furthermore, everyone must help as time was running out for them and for the Island. She told them that in order to survive they must live on the sea and come to the Island only at certain times of the year to collect food and water. She told them that only the women were allowed to do this and that the males, being responsible for the tower, could never again set foot on the Island that they had decimated.

She told the males that a terrible fate would befall them, and the Island, should they ever set foot on it again. She told them that the Great Spirit was no more on the summit of the mountain than beyond the horizon of the sea and that that was where they should seek their destiny.

'Despite their feelings of guilt and the fact that she had used an ancient form of mass hypnosis, in later years some of the males of that generation did land on the Island again. But they returned to the male rafts insane and soon gave their bodies to the sea. Eventually there were no more attempts. Meanwhile, left to its own devices, the Island began to recover. The raft people, fed by the women, also recovered and eventually flourished.

'Come Indra, I will show you the pictures of this — the ancient history of your people in the Cave of Echoes.'

Without a word Indra followed Aaron into the great chamber of the cave. In the flickering oil lamplight, the ancient cave pictures came alive. The most breathtaking pictures of all were of the calling of Sumi. These murals, looked at on the cave walls overhanging the water, appeared to have been painted upside down. Indra looked inquiringly at her friend. Smiling, Aaron pointed to the perfectly still water, caught in a great lip of rock below these images. Gazing at the surface of the water, Indra saw the beauty of the paintings reflected in the water the right way up. The only way to view this unusual art form was to look at the reflection in the pool below.

'Oh!' cried Indra, her eyes bright with tears at the ephemeral quality of these watery reflections caught in the lamplight. Aaron gently put her index finger into the water. Slowly, the ripples moved the reflections and Indra could almost imaging herself there amongst the people of those ancient times, so real did the images seem when they moved in the depths of the water.

'Your story will be here one day, Indra.' Aaron's mellifluent voice echoed deeply in the cave.

Indra felt privileged that she should be shown these murals of such beauty and antiquity, locked away in darkness, until now only seen by successive yeti women. Suddenly homesick, Indra longed for the sight and smell of the sea. But she took comfort in the constant swaying movement of the Island, like a raft beneath her. Finally they left the Cave of Echoes, silently returning to the fire to sleep.

Awakening

Indra awoke with a start. Something was wrong, her nerves were at screaming point. A great nameless panic took hold of her. She felt herself going hot, her ears were burning. The next moment she was shivering uncontrollably. She had never felt such fear. Suddenly, with a sensation that she was falling from a very great height, she realised what was missing. The Island had stopped moving. The Island was sinking, falling into the sea.

'No! No-o-o!'she screamed, clutching the floor of the cave. Prostrate in abject vertigo her head was spinning.

Aaron ran to her friend's side. 'What is it, Indra? What's the matter?'

It took a few minutes for Indra to steady herself enough to speak. Panting with fear and gasping between breaths, Indra said, 'The Island — it's stopped moving. It's sinking!'

Aaron massaged her friends taut limbs as she spoke. 'Indra, Indra, my friend, the Island never moves. The Island is always still. It is because you live on the sea that it seems to you to move. You feel it move because the rafts are always moving under you. When you come to the Island for your provisions it feels to you as if the Island moves. It does not. It is the fluid inside your ears that is still in motion. But you have stayed on the Island for some days now and the fluid in your ears has stopped moving. Now you perceive the true stillness of the Island.'

After hours of massage and reassurance, Indra began to get accustomed to the strange sensation of the stillness of the Island. It unnerved her so badly that she could think of nothing but returning to the sea.

She crawled over to her friend. She still could not feel able to walk.

Aaron was holding up a strange stone that glowed with an inner light. She turned to Indra. 'Yes it is time for you to return to the sea. Tomorrow is the festival of the Baja whales. Many are already in the lagoon. The women are anchoring their rafts along the shoreline. Darkness is falling. I will take you to the Sacred Cave. We must prepare now for the long journey through the mountain. I know that you are the one who has been chosen. Fear not, for although you will know great sadness you will also know great joy. Be at peace, my friend.'

Aaron handed Indra an earthenware cup of warm tea of herbs. Gradually Indra felt calmer as she sat watching her tall graceful friend prepare for their shadowy journey through the cave system.

Finally, with two great bags slung diagonally across her body, Aaron tied rainbow silk thread through the hollowed rock formation by a small opening in the cave wall. Indra had never noticed it before. Indicating the thread, Aaron said, 'If I should decide to return this way, I shall use this as a marker. Deep inside the mountain old routes can get blocked or changed, so although I know the way, our route may be uncertain.'

One by one she blew out the oil lamps on their ledges and threw sand on the fire. She took the last two lamps and gave one to Indra who, because of her attack of vertigo, stumbled across the cave with an ungainly walk, like that of a newborn deer. Together they left, their lights receding further and further into the hidden passageway as the cave gradually resumed it's original dark silence.

Commingled

Indra was elated at the thought of returning to the sea and looked forward to taking part in the whale song festival. Over the years she had been moved to take part several times. Women who felt called would dive into the sea and float around the motionless whales, feeling their vibrations and strange deep melodies. They would join in an ethereal communion of whales and women. Indra longed for the freedom and rhythm of the sea. The uncanny stillness of the Island beneath her feet nauseated her. As did the oppressive walls of cold rock through which they passed.

The journey through the mountain seemed endless. Indra began to wonder if Aaron was lost. Maybe they would never reach the freedom of the waves. Dizzily closing her eyes, she saw colourful fronds of seaweed waving in the current. Then, seeing the flickering light and strange rocky shadows of her present circumstance she let out a long moan.

She slumped against the tunnel wall. 'I can't go on. I can't breathe.'

Aaron turned to her. 'I will carry you, Indra, if you wish. I can see the opening to the last cavern. It is a very special place. We will rest there. After that it is only a very short distance to the Sacred Cave.'

Exhausted, Indra allowed herself to be carried to the cavern, she felt like a broken doll. She felt as if nothing could revive her spirits, but she was unprepared for the wonders of natural underground artistry. She had been resting her head against Aaron's shoulder as she was being carried. Unexpectedly she felt a breeze and heard the sound of the sea. Looking up she saw the glowing cave adorned with multicoloured stalactites and stalagmites. A phosphorescent sea was swelling gently as if taking breath. It was edged by a shore of silver sand.

A distant waterfall tumbled down the cave wall into a small pool that became a rushing torrent which bubbled and foamed across the smooth white rocks that seemed to spill with the water into the underground sea.

'So beautiful....' murmured Indra gazing at the softly lit cathedral cave.

Indra felt unable to resist the call of the underground sea. After moments resting on the sand she was wading through the shallows towards the phosphorescent deep. Each movement of her body caused light waves around her. She did not swim but floated gently, entranced by the magical wonder of the strangely lit water.

'Beautiful,' she murmured in hushed tones. When she emerged from the water Aaron wrapped her in a large rainbow silk cloth.

'You come prepared!' she smiled up at the yeti woman's face feeling rather like a small child.

'Rest now, Indra,' soothed Aaron as they sat together by the stream. Indra, still cradled in the vastness of her companion's arms, sipped the clear mountain water from the earthenware cup Aaron had produced from one of her great shoulder bags. The other bag hung limply at her side, almost empty now of the rainbow silk that had marked their progress through the heart of the mountain. The fresh sparkling water that they sipped was delicious and invigorating. The sight and sound of the sea produced in Indra a profoundly soothing peace and gradually she drifted off into a deep and dreamless sleep.

When she awoke some hours later, wrapped in the folds of Aaron's cloak, Indra saw that Aaron was standing motionless by the shore, staring into the darkest recesses of the last cave. A strange, high keening sound broke from Aaron's lips, a keening that washed around the cave walls, multiplying the sound before the diminishing reverberations dimmed and commingled into the sound of rushing water.

Aaron turned to Indra. She looked radiantly happy. 'He comes to us, my friend, your time approaches. I could not tell you of this before because I did not know that you were to meet him in this place, but he has turned towards us. I have just answered his call. The Great Whale approaches the Island.' Aaron strode towards Indra, smiling. For a few moments they hugged each other.

'Now to practicalities,' said Aaron, reaching into her bag. 'We must eat of everything I have brought. It may be a long while before we eat again.'

As she talked she set out many beautiful thinly worked gold silver, and earthenware pots. Each was small and exquisitely different from the others. She unclasped every container carefully and ceremonially. When they were all set out on the sand, each one contained a small portion of dried food, paste or sauce. Finally, she took from her bag some thin flat crisp disks with which they proceeded to eat by dipping them in paste or sauce and sprinkling them with pinches of dried food. Each mouthful was deliciously different from any food Indra had ever eaten.

Taking in anew the beauty of the muted light of the cavern as she ate, Indra felt an air of wild anticipation. She asked Aaron to tell her more about what was to happen. Aaron had become extremely excited and animated. Indra too, felt elation and full of energy, colours began to look brighter.

'What's happening to us, Aaron? I feel wonderful.'

'Whales are pure love, Indra. I do not know what will happen. Whales are wild.' She laughed, her eyes sparkling with excitement. 'I think we are feeling the telepathic emanations of his love.'

Indra felt a growing sense of great excitement and anticipation as they ate and laughed together in the last cave. The more they ate, the more intoxicated and exhilarated the two of them became until, finally, they finished their meal and Aaron suggested that Indra should bathe again in the underground sea. Indra had been longing to do so ever since she woke up and had only been waiting for the meal to end. She jumped up, slipped the shawls from her shoulders and waded into the warm silvery water. She looked back over her shoulder at Aaron. 'Aren't you coming in?' she asked.

'It is not my element, Indra — It is yours and it is the whales. I will wait here for your return.' But Indra had not waited for Aaron's reply. She plunged into the water, scattering the phosphorescent light as she swam through the semi darkness of the over hanging rock folds. Once in the sea Indra was released from great tension. A tension she did not know she was holding. The days on land had been so alien to her. To be again in the cradle of the sea was like regaining childhood. Quite suddenly her eyes brimmed with tears of relief which ran down her cheeks to link with the sea which had formed them, through the evolutionary waterways of time.

When her tears ran dry, Indra swam underwater for a while, savouring the rhythm of her totally immersed body. Indra had always delighted in underwater swimming. It was truly swimming, she felt, to swim like a whale, to dive deep only coming up for air at the last minute. To swim on the surface divided the swimming sensation -part air part water — dissatisfying. To swim underwater was a totally sensual experience. Indra swam deep under water with long rhythmic movements, her body lithe as a dolphin. As a child she had always swum underwater unlike the children and adults around her who seemed to enjoy surface swimming. From childhood she could create an under wave breath-space within her mind and body in which no effort was required. She could enjoy this blissful immersive state for a very long time. When she broke through the surface sometime later she realised she was in another part of the cavern.

Far from being dismayed by this, Indra felt a deep sense of calm well-being. She felt she lay on a great bubble on the water, a bubble from which emanated an eternal peace. She lay there in the water staring up into the luminous rock formations on the ceiling of the unknown cave. She was adrift from Aaron, separated from her people by days and a plethora of new experience. Yet she had never been more alive. Never felt such a deep and heartfelt joy. It was as if her mind had begun to encounter some larger entity, a being beyond the limits of human understanding.

A low sound reverberated around the cave like a distant thunder interspersed with long lightening call sounds which grew louder with every minute that passed. Indra felt a detached interest in this new phenomenon. The elation that was happening inside her mind and body was of far more interest to her than what was happening around her. Also she knew the sound, if she had cared to relate it to past experience. It was whale song.

Indra found herself keying into the enormity of the sound that reverberated within her and around her, sound that began to fill the cave. She, too, opened her mouth wide and sang with the whale, emulating the whale's notes with her own deep throated orgasmic resonance.

She vibrated both physically and vocally, her body shivered with pleasurable anticipation. The feeling of elation was growing stronger when, from under her floating, palpitating body she felt the warmth of contact with the whale below her, supporting and lifting her fragile body with his leviathan strength. Full contact with the whale brought Indra to full and heady ecstasy. Her shuddering cries entwined with the whales reverberating song that spanned the seas of the world. Their commingled sound radiated from them through both caverns and waters deep.

Indra felt suffused with light and sound in a profound joy that was both physical and mental. Suddenly, just as she was feeling that she would faint away with pleasure, the whale song faded. She lay panting on the whale, then she started to laugh hugely. It was the deepest, most healing unstoppable laughter. Leaning over she saw the whales eye below her and collapsed into helpless giggles, tears streaming down her face. Through the echoes of her mirth, she began to hear another voice laughing with her. It sounded like the voice of her first bond man, Dalon, only richer and deeper. She stopped laughing and looked around her.

'No, he is not here.' said the quasi familiar voice. 'I am using your memory of his voice to communicate with you. Whales have much telepathy and we are adept at sound, so I am using a synthesis of your memory of your bond man's voice with my own sound vibration and telepathy.'

As he talked Indra felt waves of love emanating from the whale. She had the strangest sensation that she had known him all her life. The Way of the Whale was her people's greatest legend — a legend of healing and sustenance and sacrificial love.

'Thank you for explaining it to me' Indra smiled.

'There is much more to explain,' laughed the whale.

'I'm sure there is!' laughed Indra with an easy familiarity, strange in such an unusual circumstance. She was beginning to feel shivering stabs of excitement at the thought of more to come.

'Well, we can't get down to business until we have cooled our passion, my love.' Whispered the whale in a seductive, almost dangerous, tone.

Sensuously, Indra turned over onto her front, arms spread as if to hug the whales great grey body. She rested her cheek against the warm taut skin.

'We are going to dive, my love' Put your hand over my blow hole.' The blow hole closed over Indra's hand, holding her firmly.

'Take your deepest breath, Indra,' he whispered.

Slowly the whale sank and the water closed over Indra's head. Down, down they went together, the water getting colder and colder until the sinking feeling stopped. They lay there in the depths in perfect stillness. For a long sensual moment the whale sent waves of ultra sound washing through Indra's extending arching body.

They rose from the depths together higher and faster, gaining momentum. Indra surrendered herself to the waves of fabulous excitement. Water pounded against her body as they surged upwards. She knew he was making love to her in the way he would with a whale partner in all but consummation. Suddenly they burst from the water together, soaring towards the high cave roof. Finally splashing down together to float laconically together. The blow hole opened. Indra kept her had there and felt the rush of warm air and water as the whale exuberantly spurted.

'Well,' laughed the whale after a delicious resting interval of mutual exploration, 'We had a time, didn't we?'

Whale-Song

'Whales are the great lovers of the world, Indra. You and I my love, exist within the all embracing love of the Way. The Way is the emanating Wave that gave birth to the stars. It is unfolding throughout time to fill the void.'

Indra lay in the shallows gazing at the dark surface of the underground sea. Her lithe body was glowing with phosphorescence. The cave reverberated with the intermittent rumbling and streaks of light-sound within the whale's voice.

'We are the fulcrum, you and I. We are at the place of energy — the moment when the wave has rolled back to its fullest extent before it starts the onward rush towards the shore and takes a breath. We are here at the point of stillness. The place in which past flow meets future flow, — the motionless moment of still water. All that comes beyond this is the forward thrust into the future, the bubbling rough and tumble of the breaking wave.'

These final words were said in tone of echoing sadness. So great was the melancholy that Indra felt two large tears fill her eyes and roll down her cheeks. She could not speak. She felt so full of love, yet deeply sad. A great compassion flooded over her. The silence lengthened.

'Is the future so sad?'

'Yes,' intoned the whale, 'It may be sad.' His voice reverberated around the cave system as if this affirmation came from a hundred places.

'It will be hard for whales to understand the actions of the sons of the raft women. In some possible or even probable futures the genocide of our nation will be long and bloody. Your people will make war on whales. Your people will not understand that when a whale is killed, a great and loving heart is lost from the world, never to return. Despite your war on us we will still love you, we cannot be otherwise. We will love you, even as the last whale swims its last lonely vigil in the last sea.'

'We could not kill!' Indra replied, distraught. 'How could it be that my people would kill you?'

'Indra, Indra, that time is far from now. Futures unfold in many different ways. We are at the place of peace, do not now distress yourself. What may be, may be. You and I alive in this special moment — this is our destiny. Swim to me Indra, we will comfort each other.'

Bathed in the warmth, comfort and love that radiated from the whale, a feeling of calm pervaded Indra's being as she again lay on the whale after their swim together.

'I believe that Aaron has told you about her ancestor, Sumi?'

'Yes,' replied Indra, rubbing her cheek against the whale, wondering at the depth of feeling she had for this creature she had met only hours ago. It was as if he had been with her all her life, perhaps in some way he had, she concluded.

'We have been aware of each others existence. You have had no direct consciousness of it, but you have known me in other ways.'

Indra smiled. It was a new sensation to have one's unspoken thought answered.

'When Aaron told you of her ancestor, Sumi,' the whale continued, 'she told you of how your people parted into male and female societies.'

'Yes' replied Indra. 'I could hardly believe this at first. We are now so completely separate except at feast times. I am only just beginning to imagine what it must have been like for us to have lived on the Island, with the males and ourselves in one location together.'

'How do you feel when the males are with you at the feast times?'

'We enjoy the time they are with us. We see our sons, they see their daughters. We have bondings with some — with others there is moon passion. It is a time of great energy and excitement when the males return. Parting is always good. There will always be other years.'

The whale sent a wave undulating between their bodies.

'Sumi was so angry that she caused the branching of the path,' the whale continued. 'Your people could no longer live on the Island. The Island needed to begin to repair the damage done by the devastating culling of its trees. If your people were to survive, provisioning visits by small groups of women were all that the Island could sustain.'

'But what has evolved over hundreds of years, from that point in time, is not what was intended. Your female society has grown soft and unquestioning. Your lack of contact with the males has caused your situation, in some ways, to remain static.'

'As the Way unfolds, your people should grow both mentally and spiritually, but now the knowledge of your past has been forgotten. Your long separation needs to be repaired. You need each other. I know this is hard for you to accept. It will not be easy for your people to welcome the males more fully into your lives at present and you must not underestimate the dangers. The males can be merciless but if you truly wish to fulfil the destiny of the human race you will need their restless energy to combine with your own imagination. You know little of the males' lives and they know little of yours. The males' lives, are impoverished by your separated state, and so too, are yours. Each of you have only the briefest glimpses. For you to live as true human beings this rift between your people and the males must be mended. You must become one people.'

Indra sat up. She felt offended and alarmed by such an outrageous idea.

'I don't understand. How could this be? It would be for our women's council to decide. Why are you telling me this?'

'Because the Great Spirit has caused a new land to be born to the north of the Island and that has changed everything. The land that has been formed is greater than this Island. The need for you to be raft people living on the ocean has now passed. The women will no longer have the power base of being gatherers and provisioners. The males will eventually find their food sources from the new land and claim their right to take it. Your people will lose a role that has been theirs for hundreds of years. The change will be devastating. A new balance must be established between the males and yourselves.'

'What do you want of me?' wailed Indra, trying to take in the enormity of what had just been revealed. She felt as if she was breaking apart under the strain of trying to comprehend it all.

'I only know that you and I are the crucible in which certain future possibilities rest. I ask only that you store these things in your heart, in love, until the knowledge you have been given is needed to help your people — all of your people.'

Indra's heart was too full to reply. She slid off the whale and swam towards the dark shore but she realised that she still needed the comfort and swell of the water around her body. She lay motionless at the waterline, gazing at the soft phosphorescent glow of the stalactites and stalagmites that paraded into the far recesses of the cave. She could feel the enormous physical presence of the whale in the deep water behind her. She became acutely aware of the warm water swirling around her body and knew that he warmed the water with his vastness. She knew that he too felt the gentle thrust and pull of the water. The whale's wild sensual energy yet high spiritual love came in wave upon wave, breaking upon her. Indra entered a prolonged state of deep orgasmic surrender. Until hours later she felt as if she lay drifting amongst the stars in the far flung corners of the universe.

Odyssey

Indra awoke in the soft glow of the cave. Aaron was sitting beside her, bathing her forehead, her white face framed by her long white hair was full of concern.

'Where is he Aaron?' groaned Indra, feeling a deep sense of loss. Her eyes scanned the empty water. She felt restless and angry.

'I must go to him!'

Indra tried to get up but her muscles felt stiff and weak. She could do nothing but fall back on the multicoloured silks of Aaron's cloak in which she was wrapped.

'You must rest, Indra.' soothed Aaron. 'You will see him again, I think, but for now you must turn the power of your mutual love inwards. You must be gentle with yourself and be at peace.'

Aaron took from her bag a silver cylinder shaped in two cones. She opened it by twisting it in the middle. She raised Indra's head so she could drink the soothing liquid from one of the cones. In the other cone were flakes of dried herbs which melted on Indra's tongue.

'Sleep now, Indra. Be safe in the knowledge of his great love for you. It was for your sake that he has left you. Prolonged contact with him would be impossible for your body to bear. Whales are pure unconditional, undiluted love. Sleep now.'

After many hours of fitful delirium, Indra heard the sound of surf breaking on the shore. Her eyes were so unaccustomed to the light that it was a few minutes before she could open them fully. When she looked round she was lying on the beach directly below the Sacred Cave. She sat up slowly, still feeling very weak. Aaron came towards her from the shadow of the overhanging rock.

'I thought the sun would heal you, Indra.' I cannot stay long out here, I need to return to the cool of the mountain as you feel the need to return to the sea. I have summoned Twoclickslong to help you. You can see him out there waiting for you. He will take you to your people and the world you know. Conserve your strength and do not yet talk of the truths that you know. When the time is ripe you will know it. The wave begins to roll towards the shore.'

She pulled Indra to her feet. She looked gently down at Indra from her great height and for a long moment they held each other's hands, gazing into each others eyes.

'Goodbye, my friend.' Her great orchestral voice was muted to a sad oboe.'

Indra reached up and kissed Aaron's cheek which Aaron returned. They heard a splash and turned to see a slim dolphin somersaulting skywards.

'Now you must return to the sea and I to the mountain. My work here is done.'

While Aaron strode up the cliff path towards the folds of rock at the entrance of Sacred Cave, Indra waded out towards the open sea. The sunshine and the sea air were already putting new life into her. The thought of returning to the rafts lifted her spirits. The dolphin began to swim playfully towards her. Suddenly it disappeared.

Moments later Indra felt an insistent nudging at the back of her legs. As she lost her balance the dolphin rose beneath her. His wild energy was surging between her legs. Regaining her balance she grabbed his dorsal fin. The dolphin, a total expression of a creature able to tap into earth's flowing energy, lay motionless for a moment to allow its human cargo to adjust herself on his back.

Indra turned briefly towards the shore and waved to Aaron who stood at the entrance of the sacred cave. Aaron gave an answering wave with both arms held high. Her multicoloured cloak billowing like a sail in the wind. Indra replaced her hand on the dolphin's fin and they were off, cutting through the waves. The power of the dolphin's body and the exhilarating speed at which they travelled commanded Indra's full attention. Churning through the waves she hugged the dolphin close, half riding half lying along its back, clinging to the dorsal fin as they surged in and out of the wind and water at breathtaking speed. Yet Indra sensed that the powerful creature was moving gently for her. That she bore witness to only part of his potential strength.

After only a short while she caught sight of the raft system, lit by brilliant shafts of light from strands of stormy sunset clouds.

Resting her cheek against its flank, she gave thanks. She was almost home.

Breaking the Mould

The aromatic wood of her raft greeted Indra like the scent of a lover returning. The familiar boards beneath her feet seemed to give her the profound relief of an expert masseuse. Indra felt tears of relief well up into her eyes as she entered her hut feeling for the spark of flint to light the oil lamp. In the dim flickering of the lamp she took off her dripping silk tunic, dried herself quickly, and got into bed. Time enough in the morning for welcoming parties.

She listened to the distant voices of the women and children going to their rest. Tired though she was, she could not seem to drift off to sleep. The excitement of her return seemed unfulfilled. She almost wished now that she had made her presence known to her neighbours. The rise and fall of the raft system at anchor kept her awake. She had never realised that the rafts moved quite so much. She could not get used to it again. She had been on still land for too long. Finally she got up, tied three shawls around herself against the chilled night air, blew out her oil lamp and left her hut.

Indra stood outside. There was a still oppressive dry atmosphere but the storm itself was yet distant — maybe two days off. That was why they had not yet run for the Island, she concluded. A flying fish flopped onto her raft, wriggling and writhing in the agony of air. Not wishing to watch its moonlit death, she walked across the connecting bridge to the next raft — the water-nut raft —and chopping the top off one nut, she drank her fill. Realising she was in fact quite hungry Indra crossed the bridge to the agri-raft and ate some sprouting alfalfa and beans.

When hunger and thirst had been assuaged she decided to give votive thanks to the Great Spirit for her safe return. She began to make her starlit journey towards the largest raft — the theatre raft where her people held their feasts and services. It was linked to the Inner Sanctum where no man was ever allowed.

Indra crossed the little known link bridge from the agri-raft to the back of the theatre raft. It was a link bridge that she herself had made to facilitate her journey to the theatre where she spent many of her waking hours devising dances and mimes, painting masks and designing backdrops and costumes. The women sometimes referred to it as "Indra's second home." Again the scents of memory wafted through the still night air as she crossed the theatre floor. Slowly and reverently, feeling the ancient carvings beneath her feet, Indra crossed the bridge to the Inner Sanctum.

Indra could see the glow of light that was always kept burning through the tall archway. The beautiful silk canopy billowed slightly as if it was breathing. The poised, small breasted, exquisite statue gazed down at her. Indra reached up, as if she longed to embrace the ancient image. Silently she gave thanks for her safe return. After some time she began remembering all that had happened on the Island. In sacred prayer she asked questions, begging for some sign as to when and how she was to impart her newfound knowledge to her people. Perhaps it was because of the ferment her mind was in that she could not hear the answers given. Maybe there were no answers. There seemed to be nothing but silence emanating from the beautiful wooden image, except perhaps a gentle smile of deep compassion.

After a while Indra felt disappointed and dropped her arms. She had become almost used to something special happening to her. She had felt sure that she would be shown some new insight or knowledge that night. Perhaps the message is that I should embody more peace within, she thought as she crossed the bridge back to the theatre.

She felt enormously tired and started yawning and stretching, almost uncontrollably. She remembered the pile of soft background silks she sometimes rested on, behind the stage. Now, hardly able to put one heavy foot in front of the other, she remembered that Aaron had told her to rest. She wished that she had taken her advice because she was beginning to feel rather sick and faint. At last she flopped down, rolling into the pile of silks and slept.

*   *   *

When Indra awoke the next day she felt decidedly unwell. Her mouth was dry, her chest tight and she knew she was feverish. 'Leacia will have to give me some healing medicine,' she thought. 'I'd better call someone to help me.' There was a buzzing in her ears. The buzzing resolved itself and she realised it was urgent conversation, almost as if there was an argument — but something was different.

Just then she heard several males shouting at each other, then girls voices giggling and shushing them, quite close to her.

That is no way to be behaving so close to the Inner Sanctum, thought Indra crossly. Why are the males here? Is it feast time? Have I been away so long?

She thought she could hear her daughter's voice. 'Mione?' she called out weakly. She was greeted by complete silence. Did I dream the voices? Am I so very feverish?

'Mione!' she called again. This time her call was greeted by running footsteps. Indra lay back with relief.

'Indra! How did you get here? Have you been hiding here all this time? How did you know of our plan?'

It was Suyra, her sister's daughter who spoke. She was a few years older than Mione and Indra had confused their voices. Perhaps she had had some loss of hearing due to her feverish state. She shook with chills and her head was throbbing. This was not the kind of response to her homecoming that Indra had expected. She found herself angered at Suyra's arrogant tone of voice.

Some young males arrived behind the young woman.

'Hiding?… I'm not hiding! Why would you think that? I fell asleep here… Last night I think… but maybe…longer …very thirsty…Tell your friends to take me to Leacia, I need healing medicine. I am not well.'

Suyra ignored Indra's demands. 'Do the women's council know of our plan? Are they going to follow us to the new land? Why are you here? No-one was supposed to know.'

Indra felt a sense of shock. So they knew of the new land. She had supposed this was one of the things she was to impart to the raft people at some future appointed time. She thought she had been given prior knowledge and that her role was to be that of messenger. She searched the tense young crowd for answers, then shook her head to try to get some clarity.

Have I received a sign? she thought confusedly, her skin burned and then went cold. Or have I already told them of it and do not remember?

Aloud she said, 'So you know... of the new land?'

Both the males and young women caught their breath. 'So they do know about it!' came a male voice from the back. 'They must be following us.'

Suyra looked back at her aunt. 'Do they know?' she asked Indra.

Indra closed her eyes in feverish confusion. 'Suyra please, I am sick... I need water... I do not know what is known... or what is unknown. I have only just returned to the raft system. I do not understand how you all know about the new land. I was told of it by the Great Whale.'

Suyra took half a step back. She looked at Indra with a respect and reverence that bordered on fear.

'Perhaps that is why we have seen a whale constantly shadowing the raft.'

She turned to the gathering of young people behind her. 'The whale swims with us because he knows she is here. Maybe that is all. If that is so, the whale is not an ill omen for our quest.'

'Perhaps you are right,' said a male voice from the back. 'But I don't like it, nonetheless.'

Indra started coughing. Her breath became laboured. She did not want to be surrounded by these young people asking her confusing questions. She was feeling very thirsty. She wanted to get back to her raft hut.

'Suyra, could you ask them to get me some water. Would you carry me to my raft hut and send someone to run to get Leacia. I need an infusion for my fever. I must rest now.'

Suyra looked worried. 'Indra, don't you realise we are at sea?'

'Oh well,' said Indra. 'We cannot be far from the Island now. Get her as soon as we drop anchor. Please ask everyone to go away, I want to be alone.'

'She doesn't realise.' said the girl next to Suyra. 'What are we going to do with her?'

Being referred to like this, above her head, made Indra very angry. She had been given important new knowledge to impart to the raft people. She was a member of the

Council of Women. They had no right to speak of her like this.

Summoning up her remaining strength, Indra sat up. 'You will leave me in peace until we are at anchor. The Council will have something to say to you all when I report that you young women set sail with these males still on board. They should be on their own rafts and well you know it. I have never heard of such a thing!'

'Indra, my aunt, there seems to have been a terrible mistake. I am truly sorry that you are not well. It is most unfortunate because we are not going back to the Island at all. Our generation, sworn to secrecy, have been planning this for the last week. Ever since Uwen came to us and told us of the new land that he has seen. The new land is to the north of our Island. It was from the new land that the darkness came. It is about a weeks' journey from here. We set sail secretly last night in the early hours. We took this one raft in order to stay together. So there would be no chance of our raft separating in unfamiliar seas. This was the only possible raft to take, and one of the easiest, as all of us women have sailed it back to the Island at some time. You know it is one of our generation's responsibilities to sail the theatre raft. We have set sail with the males that we may see the new land for ourselves. We plan to live on it. Together!' There were murmurs of agreement.

Indra drew in her breath sharply. 'Leave me!' she yelled, exploding into a fit of coughing. Then more softly, 'Please get me a drink, Suyra.'

'Indra, may I stay with you?' Leacia's daughter Gerda bent down and took her hand. She gave Indra sips of water from her waxed silk water pouch.

'I have a bag of medicines and powders. It is said I have healing hands.'

Indra lay back. 'Stay' she gasped weakly, and closed her eyes.

Gerda called over her shoulder. 'Thea, would you get my red silk cloak?'

Soon Gerda's cloak was brought and from its pouches and pockets medicine and powders brought relief to Indra's ills and at last, when her feet were warmed by a wrapped stone from their makeshift hearth, she slept.

While Indra slept fitfully for the next two days, the Great Whale continued to shadow the theatre raft. The males could not shake their fear of ill omen, of an impending doom incurred by the presence of the whale. Not one of the closed young minds could feel the emanations of love that radiated from the whale.

From the Great Whale's perspective everything was, in some ways, going even better than could be expected. It had been an unforeseen possibility that the young males would find the new land so soon. Let alone that the young women should decide to leap with them into the unknown. Change was certainly in the air.

The Way of the Great Spirit had influenced these young people to act in a most unconventional manner. Something else unforeseen had happened to Indra. He could feel that her energies were erratic and confused. He wished that she would get into the water so that he could know what was wrong. All he could do was send her telepathic waves of support that he knew his presence would bring her.

It was at times like these he wished that whales could see more accurately into the future that fanned out before him. Due to the monumental changes that had taken place harmonic frequencies had become jarring and off key. The water around him felt strongly and deeply disturbed by the formation of the new land. It swirled around him in a way that seemed almost menacing. Never had the water in which he lived felt so strange. To calm himself he sang an ultra beautiful day long love song, that was felt by all the whales and dolphins for thousands of miles distant.

They could hear the whale song on the raft. A grating jarring reverberation that went on all day. It unnerved them even more than the whale's silent shadowing. Their nerves already taut, the strange sound grated and set their teeth on edge.

'Why is it shadowing us?' yelled Jesson. Suyra could hear the dark anger in his voice 'Your aunt has brought us bad luck.'

'Oh, Jesson,' cried Suyra, 'It is an accident that she is with us.'

'Too right it is!' replied Jesse. 'I could kill her, and that bloody whale!'

'Jesson, don't say such things! At least the wind is in the right direction. We are making fast progress. So things can't be too bad. What if we were to become becalmed? Then I might agree they brought bad luck. But as it is we should be in sight of the new land in a few days, shouldn't we? So think about what we shall do when we get there and try to stop thinking about my aunt and the whale.'

Jesson began to walk towards the other side of the raft, Suyra walked with him.

'Some chance I have to forget about the whale when it's making that eerie racket. And the wind is too strong. We'll have to take the sail down soon or it will rip.'

'Yes this is storm wind. We'll weigh anchor and rest for a while,'replied Suyra, rather naively.

'Oh, and I suppose you'll get me some herb tea to calm my nerves — or even some soft smoke!' said Jesson sarcastically. 'Don't you realise there's no lea of the Island to protect us? We'll have to ride out the storm — and on this large raft that won't be an easy task. I don't know how it will take it. We've never handled such a large raft under storm conditions. And you've never handled it in storm conditions at all! This raft has never ridden out a storm in open sea. It's hundreds of years old. It may break apart!'

The truth of his words sunk into the young people that were grouped around him. Overhead dark clouds scudded by, pursued by a vast cloud bank. A deep purple intermingled with the swirling yellow mass. For the first time Suyra felt truly frightened. She had not voiced her own misgivings about the enormity of the impending storm she felt was in the air. This was the strange storm that had been slowly brewing ever since the northern horizon went dark. It had been fermenting in the atmosphere for weeks. The effect on the skin was dry and prickly, hair stood up on forearms. Perhaps it was even a storm madness that had goaded them into this escapade that broke with all tradition and taboo.

Since the time of Sumi, males and women had lived separate lives, apart from the feast times once a year when the male rafts visited. The women lived peaceful, uneventful lives in the calm seas around the Island, apart from the occasional storm. The women always had sufficient warning from the feel of the air, to run for the protection of the Island lagoon. They spent their lives taking short provisioning trips to the island, spinning their rainbow silks for sails, rope and clothing and weaving wonderful stories for their young. No woman had ever faced a storm out at sea.

Suyra felt herself begin to shake. She turned away from Jesson then half turned back.

'I'm going to see how Gerda is getting on with Indra. You had better take down the sail soon, before it's torn to shreds. We should be getting everyone to start packing things away and tie as much down as we can. You are right, we may not survive the oncoming storm. I'm as unnerved as you are, but it's no use us shouting at each other. Let's pass round some soft smoke to those who need it. I shall come back to help you in a while'. Suyra felt her knees almost give way as she walked behind the stage.

*　　*　　*

All night the wind screamed like a banshee through the rigging of the theatre raft which was more complex than any other raft. It had several spars holding up the massive sail, which the young women had taken down and folded away.

The young people huddled together in pairs or groups, each one watched and felt the massive seas broiling beneath the raft. Jesson and his brother, Yon, tried to steer a course through the turbulent waves in the piercing, dark rimmed brightness of the storm light.

During the night Indra had responded to Gerda's ministrations. She had taken

Valerian and had slept, despite the noise of the storm. She was much less feverish. Her chest had eased since Gerda's massage, and she only coughed now and then. Waking suddenly she heard the wind and felt a dreadful pitching of the raft. She drew comfort from the proximity of the Great Whale. She could feel the strength of the love he sent her through the churning seas and felt at peace.

Very suddenly the daylight dimmed to a murky greyness. The explosions of lightening lit up the entire sky for several minutes at a time. The raft was pitched and tossed at alarming angles in the giant waves

Then everyone onboard saw the lightning ball coming towards them. As it exploded they felt a juddering shock. The deafening thunder crash stunned them senseless. There was an enormous crack as the mast broke in two. It hit the deck, smoking. Many, included Indra, fainted with shock and all became temporarily deaf to greater or lesser degrees. A weird mime ensued. Everyone was in a state of abject terror and confusion and even Jesson and Yon had abandoned their posts. Water was slopped over the crazily tilted deck. Keeping out of the way of the slithering rigging was a nightmare. It seemed to cast about as if trying to catch something in its tentacles.

In the storm-racked hours that followed, the tangled rigging managed to knock almost everything off of the deck except the stage and a few large changing huts behind the stage. Lightening intermittently lit up the nightmare scene and thunder exploded over head but still no rain released the tension.

Almost as spectacularly as it had started, the storm died and they were becalmed in the eye of the storm. Indra called out to the scattered young males and women that there was more to come. Her voice sounded very mute and flat, almost inaudible although she knew she was shouting. Then she realised that she had been deafened by the thunderbolt. She ran to the nearest large group and indicated to them to tell the others that it was not over and that they must shelter in the changing huts or under the stage because now they could undertake to climb over the shattered rigging to comparative safety.

Indra then went to the edge of the raft to munch a dry flat bread that Gerda had thrust into her hand on her rounds to see who needed the most help and comfort.

Indra looked at the rope bridge she had made years ago trailing in the water. She felt a sudden desperate longing for the order of the raft system and her own little raft hut. She wished that she could have lived in past times and not in this ever changing turmoil of her present. She saw the whale spouting quite close and knew that she had experienced great things and that she could not really wished that it was otherwise. She felt waves of telepathic love emanating from the Great Whale. His enormous bulk glided effortlessly towards her through the choppy grey sea. Indra reached out and touched his vast flank as he gently came alongside the raft. Indra could not speak so great was her emotion at seeing him again. Forgetting everyone and everything, she rested her head close to his eye, against his towering body alongside the raft.

Gradually, despite her deafness she became aware of people shouting behind her. She looked round to see the young males and women grouped behind the stage looking very angry and hostile. Most of the males were holding broken spars from the mast. Jesson and some other young men held part of the mast-head like a battering ram. The long broken point was aimed at the whale's flank which was hard up against the side of the raft.

'What are you doing?' she asked. Her voice did not have the commanding tone she intended, instead it sounded weak and frightened. She realised this was partly because of her deafness. Looking at them she realised that they too, afflicted by deafness, had hardly heard her. It was as if everything had been slowed down, and yet part of her knew that things were happening very fast.

In her half-silent world they ran towards the whale clutching their jagged weapons. They looked as if an ugly madness had taken possession of them. It was as if they believed the whale to be in some way responsible for the dreadful storm. She saw, too in that slow split second, that they hated her unexpected presence on the raft, that she too was a focus for their hatred. She was part of the old world they wished to leave behind, part of the tradition that they had broken in their daring escapade. They were intent of giving vent to their fear and anger.

'No!' she cried, as the mast rammed home, deep into the whale's side. The blood spurted out in a great fountain, covering the attackers and turning their madness into a horrific image, as if they had become writhing, bloody entrails as the force of the impact sent them reeling, slipping and sliding on the deck of the theatre raft amongst the slithering ropes.

Indra felt an explosion of pain and light before she sank, unconscious, into a disturbing darkness.

Is Land

Indra sat up, her head splitting. She felt a trickle of blood running down her cheek. She reached up and realised her hair was caked with blood. She felt very weak and shaky. She licked her dry flaked lips, she was very thirsty. Looking slowly around her she saw the Great Whale quite close to her on the rocky shore, the broken mast sticking out of his side. Unable to walk, she crawled painfully towards him in the dimming light and shooed away the birds that had gathered around him. When she reached him she rested her head gently against his drying flank. His tail flicked weakly in the receding surf and with a surge of hope she realised he was not dead. She tried to send love to him and felt his love wash back into her being. She knew he still loved her people despite the pain they had caused him. She knew his love was universal, unconditional and constant. With a long lingering goodbye she felt his great body shudder and his spirit was gone. Surrendered to the stars.

Indra's surroundings mirrored her desolation. She was totally alone except for the curious birds that waited to gorge themselves on the vast feast before them. The effort of her latest exertions proved too much for Indra and she again slipped into unconsciousness as she lay bereft on the lonely shore.

*   *   *

Gerda bent over the limp form lying beside the whale. The small group had been foraging along the shore when they had seen the white birds wheeling around the distant form of the beached whale.

'We must take her back to camp. She will soon die if we leave her out in this sun.'

'I think we should leave her here,' said Jesson. 'The whale must have brought her here from the eye of the storm. She must be a shaman of great power.'

'And that is why we must take care of her,' replied Gerda. 'Her power may be useful to us. We cannot overshadow this new land with her death. If we walk away now it will be as if we killed her. The Great Spirit brought us here and brought her with us. We have done an evil thing in killing the whale. The strange storm confused us and made us mad. To leave Indra here, one of our own people, to let her die without even trying to save her now, could cause the Great Spirit to turn Her back on us. It was Her will that Indra did not drown. She has given us another chance. For the sake of our future here we must take Indra back to camp.'

I agree with Gerda,' agreed Suyra. 'I could not leave my kinswoman here to die. Jesson, you cannot ask it of me. We will take her back immediately.'

'But you don't understand. She knows we tried to kill her.'

'Yes she knows, and she may yet die. If she lives it will be because the Great Spirit has willed it.'

The sad little procession made its way towards a geyser of hot fresh water spurting up into the air. It was the only feature in the barren landscape. The remains of the theatre raft had been washed up above the shoreline of a little inlet into which the geyser water flowed.

The young people that had not joined the search party were already forming a number of crude tipi constructions using wood from the raft together with bits of torn sail and a few rocks. Some shelters merely made use of fissures in the warm rock which were then covered by a pieces of silk sail held down by rocks on the surface. Indra was placed in one of the latter dwelling places, watched over by Gerda.

The young people sat round the scant driftwood fire that evening, cooking eggs that had been found on various expeditions during the day. Suyra had found a small amount of edible seaweed which was also now cooking. A great hunk of whale meat, skewered by a long thin spar, was being spit roasted by a young male. The others watched, almost mesmerised by the rhythmic turning of the dripping, spitting succulent soft meat.

'Look at the light that comes from dripping fat. We can make oil lamps from that.'

There was silence around the fire for a while, eyes stared into the hot flames. Some were willing the future to hold promise, some were feeling the loneliness of the new land, some were longing for the comforting swell of the raft system.

'I'm hungry, Jesson. When will it be cooked?'

'I think it's ready now. Who's got the cutting shell?'

Hungrily they took their food back to their places by the fire.

'This is good,' mumbled Yon, through his mouthful of food. The others nodded their heads in agreement, their mouths too full to answer with anything more than grunts of affirmation. Eating whale meat was a rare occurrence. Only occasionally did male rafts encounter dead whales at sea. Rarely did one beach itself on the Island to be harvested by the raft women.

When they had eaten their fill Gerda got up.

'I will take some to Indra' she said skewering a small piece. 'It will make her stronger.'

'Do you think she will eat it?' asked Suyra.

'She is too weak to notice what she is eating, but if she does eat the meat it will help her recovery. I think I must try to give her some.'

Several of the young people had small musical instruments that had survived the storm, tucked away in the folds of their silk robes. They now started to play together. Those that did not have instruments clapped their hands or tapped the rock with their wooden skewers. Later still, as the fire dwindled, someone sang as they drifted off to their shelters for the night.

The sea gurgled and crashed against the rocky shore. It seemed as if the sea had lost its rhythm and it emitted a confused and sloppy sound which was somewhat disconcerting to those who listened, subliminally it jarred their nerves. No-one slept particularly well that night. Indra tossed and turned feverishly in her warm rocky hollow, her head felt as if it was breaking in two. She felt haunted by the knowledge that she had forgotten something and she also knew that remembering whatever it was would be unbearably painful. She dreamed that she was searching for a vast monster, an unknown horror that kept lurking just under her raft. She was constantly aware of an odd taste in her mouth. One moment she thought she liked the taste, the next she would feel nauseated.

Gerda cared for her constantly as Indra drifted feverishly between sleeping and waking. Her recurring nightmare was that she was falling down a dark hole. It was a terrifying sensation. Whenever she recognised Gerda she would cling to her, shivering and crying to be taken home, as if she were a small child. Gerda felt out of her depth, the head wound was healing slowly and Indra should be recovering. What was it that frightened her so?

Ayly caught up with Suyra as they walked along the rocky shore towards the whales carcass. 'Is Indra any better today, Suyra?' Ayly had always admired Suyra and sought the security of her company. She felt rather afraid of the grey rocky landscape and she had not enjoyed her first nights on the new land.

'Gerda says that the signs are not good but she is taking a little food and water, so there is still some hope for her recovery.'

Fermentation

Jesson called to them as they approached the great hulk. 'Come quickly you two, we need all the help we can get!' He ran along the beach shooing away the white birds that were gathering on and around the beached whale.

'We must save as much as we can before they eat it all. We could cut and dry enough for a years supply if we work fast. Some of us are planning to make camp here so that we can guard it. This whale meat could be our salvation!'

'If you are going to camp here we must bring you water. What about fuel for the fire? Shall we bring some wood from the raft?'

'I don't think we will need it. Just come and look at this.'

He led Suyra and Ayly inland from the shore 'This land is full of wonder. Her Spirit is surely with us.'

As they walked over a layer of orange rock, Suyra smelt a strange smell. Walking a little further they were aware of the increased warmth of the rock beneath their feet. Looking over the edge of a yellow rock they saw a small spitting fire burning. It looked as if the rock itself burned and yet did not blacken.

'What is it?' asked Suyra. 'How does the rock burn? This is surely a miracle.'

'I think it has something to do with this strange smell. It seems to come from the rock itself. I think that beneath this land there is a great fire that warms the rock and this small fire spit is part of it.'

'How did you find it?'

'I was searching for something to keep the birds away.'

'It was surely the Great Spirit's hand that led you here.'

'Ayly, you go back to the whale and help Jesson with the meat. I will go back to our camp and bring some water.'

'Yes, that is a good idea. We are getting thirsty. Bring as many people as you can to help us.'

Suyra felt elated as she ran back to the camp. Everything was going so well. That morning she had begun to realise their mad impetuosity in setting off for the new land. It had all seemed so exciting to plan to take the theatre raft and be the first to explore. It had seemed right to set off with the males of their generation, secretly provisioning the theatre raft for their trip. How surprised the women's council would be when they returned to tell of the adventure. But now they could not return, the theatre raft was beached and beyond repair. Being stuck on the new land had not been a part of their plan. Now they would have to live here and make the best of it until a male raft found them. This new land was full of surprises and possibilities. The strange rock fire was a wonderful blessing. If only the fresh water spring was nearer the fire. They would have to become two camps, the raft-water camp and the whale-fire camp, until the whale meat was all dried.

The hot sun beat down on Suyra as she made her way towards the spurting geyser. When she had drunk her fill of the foul tasting tepid water that would nonetheless quench her thirst Suyra called the others to her.

'We must all go and help Jesson to cut up the whale. If we work quickly we will have food enough to last us long. Jasse has discovered a gift from the Great Spirit's heart. She has given us Her fire — it comes from within the rock without needing wood. Some of us must make a new camp there. I have decided to stay there with Jesson and the rest of you must decide what you will do. We must bring water enough for us, for a day's work.'

'How are we going to take water to them? Most of the containers were broken in the storm.'

'Bring me anything which could contain water. Search the raft again — there must be something we could use.'

A sorry collection of small containers were brought to the geyser, none of them big enough to carry a substantial amount of water.

Caley came forward and shyly whispered something to Suyra. 'Caley,' cried Suyra. 'I think that's the answer!' She hugged the younger girl. 'How clever of you. Tell them what you just told me.'

Shyly, Caley looked round her group of friends.

'Well, when I went to the raft to look for water holders I noticed a sail trailing in the water. It held the water within it and I wondered if we could use the waxed sail to carry the water, if we all held part of the sail all the way round, most of the water would not fall out. Then, when we reach the fire, perhaps we can find a hollow — like the one I used for shelter last night — and lower the sail into it, to hold the water in.

Knowing how shy Caley was, Suyra put her arm around her again. 'I think it's a wonderful idea.'

'Yes' called Imba, who was Caley's special male friend. 'Caley often has good ideas!' Amid general ribaldry Imba made his way through the group and took her hand. He looked at her lovingly for a moment then hand in hand they led the group towards the battered raft.

The young people quickly freed the sail from the tangle of ropes. They carried it to the geyser and the sail was soon brimming with the fresh warm water. It was very heavy and everyone was needed to carry it along the shoreline. Gerda left Indra in order to help them. She was intrigued by the idea of the rock fire and wanted to see this new miracle for herself. Indra was sleeping and her fever seemed to be abating a little.

By the time they were in sight of the whale the water carriers were very tired. Suyra ran ahead to get Jesson and Ayly to help them. They found a suitable hollow in the rock and lowered the sail into it to hold the water.

When they had all refreshed themselves and Caley had again been congratulated on her clever idea, they all went to inspect the rock fire phenomenon. As they approached they saw the whale meat spread out on the rocks beside the spitting fire. They all stood silently for a few minutes gazing at the hypnotic flames.

'We must give thanks to Great Spirit as the sun sets. She has shown us her heart here in this new land,' intoned Suyra.

Solemnly the women hugged each other, then the males. This new and bounteous miracle dispelled any last doubts that Her Spirit was with them. Everyone was filled with great hope and happiness.

'Now you must all help me to bring more whale meat here — we need your cutting shells.' said Jesson. 'Tonight we will use this fire to cook our meal. Chenio, come here, I want you to go back to the raft in a while and get something. It's a surprise, so don't ask me anymore. Suyra you take the others to the whale we need to keep the white birds away or they will take it all. I'll follow in a moment.'

By early evening a substantial amount of whale meat was piled on the rocks around the fire to dry.

After the young women had woven their circle dance of thanksgiving, they all sprawled themselves on the warm rocks waiting for the whale meat that was cooking on a spar from the theatre raft. They were all very hungry and the meat smelled good. Gerda felt a little guilty that she had left Indra alone for so long. She resolved to return to her after the meal and take some food. Chenio had told her that Indra was still sleeping peacefully when he had returned.

'Come on, Chenio,' called Imba, from the high rock where he and Caley were lounging. 'What is Jesson's surprise?'

Chenio reached into a hollow in the rock beside him and brought out a large object wrapped in silk to reveal a great round gourd. The young men instantly recognised the meaning of the gourd and cheered.

The women were mystified by their exuberance.

'Why have your brought that? Why are you all cheering? We don't understand,' called Suyra.

Jesson walked over to her and pulled her to her feet. 'Come with me Suyra, you will soon understand.' The males laughed and watched Jesson take Suyra towards Chenio who held the gourd between his legs.

Chenio was a squat, dark, rather hairy young man. Jesson's stature was tall and commanding, as was Suyra's, though she only reached to Jesson's shoulder. Watching the little scene, everyone realised how bespattered with whale blood they all were. It bordered on the macabre to watch the tall bloodied male bring his smaller bloodied female towards Chenio who hugged the gourd with dark blood-red hands.

A unexpected silence fell and with a slight chill breeze a shiver ran through the assembled group.

Chenio unstopped the gourd. 'Let's see how well it travelled, shall we?' He poured the liquid into a shell cup and offered it first to Jesson, who held it aloft to show the other males.

'Smells good,' he called, then drained the cup. 'Let Suyra try some.'

Again Chenio filled the shell.

'Suyra, this will make you feel good, then you will understand why we males are cheering.'

Suyra took the cup. She had never smelt anything like it. She took an experimental sip. It tasted sweet and warmed her throat. She drank a little more.

'What is it, Suyra?' called Gerda.

'I don't know what it is, but it tastes sweet — Jesson what is it?' As she gazed questioningly into Jesson's eyes she realised that she was experiencing a strange physical sensation. She knew she wanted to be with him and felt a strong surge of moon passion but there was something more, there was something unexpectedly urgent about this feeling — something that made her feel wanton and unrestrained. She felt dizzy. Jesson bent down and kissed her and instead of drawing away with her normal reserve, she threw caution to the wind and kissed him back with her whole body pressing sensuously against his. She didn't care that there were people around her. She slid slowly down his body onto the rock below, invitingly pulling him down towards her.

'What's in that stuff?' Gerda called. She was shocked by such an overt display of sensuality. Bonded couples were rarely demonstrative in public. Holding hands and kissing lightly was as far as things went. Bonding took place behind closed raft doors. Suyra and Jesson looked almost as if they were in the act of bonding in front of everyone. What had happened to Suyra, Gerda wondered, that she looked so different.

'Don't worry, Gerda.' said Chenio, grinning. 'I'll bring you some right now. I think I'd better leave this rock to the two of them anyway.'

Amid the general laughter of the males Chenio came over to Gerda, hugging the large gourd to his chest. He poured himself a cup then gave one to Gerda. 'It'll make you see things differently, Gerda, try some.'

Cautiously Gerda sipped.

'It's fermented drink, isn't it?' she asked.

'Yes,' replied Chenio. 'You've got its measure.'

'Suyra!' called Gerda helplessly. 'What should we do?'

But there was no reply. Suyra and Jesson were lying on the rock, entwined together, totally engrossed. Jesson was caressing Suyra's breast, her shawls were draped carelessly across the rock. Suyra's hands gripped his shoulders. They had not yet stopped kissing.

The others looked on fascinated. None of the young women had been with a male before, although some of the males had had bondings with older women.

Chenio looked quizzically at Gerda and within that look was something of arrogance and appraisal. Gerda did not like him looking at her in that way.

'Go,' she said dismissively. 'Take it away.'

She got up and turned the meat on spit above the fire. She felt a deep sense of disquiet.

The fermented drink was something beyond her experience, her throat felt on fire although she had only taken a small sip. By the time she turned to the others the drink had been handed round. Everyone looked relaxed and happy, several couples were kissing and Caley was giggling.

Gerda felt isolated. She was outside their happy euphoria. The fermented drink had changed something deep and fundamental. The women no longer held their natural dignity. The old order was changed, this was a new order in a new world. Gerda felt her inner security and serenity challenged. She felt dirty and whale bloody. She decided that she would stay no longer. She cut two large hunks of whale meat off the spit and set off along the shore towards the theatre raft. The sound of the surf soon drowned out the sounds of merriment from the whale fire camp.

Gerda felt glad to be alone with the sea and stars. Suyra's behaviour had shocked her and she knew that most of the other young women would follow her lead. Women had never drunk the fermented drink until today. It had only been the stuff of legend, a whispering about the strange things the males did on their own.

Now they all had drunk and it had changed them. This was a new weaving pattern, a new dye in the silk of the Great Spirit's weaving.

Gerda washed off the blood in the stream that ran from the geyser to the sea. She wrapped herself in a silk costume from a store that had survived the storm and walked towards Indra's hollow. From the rocks she heard Indra calling.

'I'm coming, Indra!' she shouted above the noise of the waves.'

Carefully she got down between the rocks. With a spark rock she lit the tinder and then the stubby candle she had used the night before.

'Oh, Indra. I am sorry that I left you so long. You were asleep and the others needed help. How are you feeling?'

'Better for seeing you, Gerda.' For a few minutes they held each other tightly in the greeting form.

'You feel much stronger, Indra. Is your fever gone?'

'Yes, thanks to your ministrations I feel myself again. You are truly a healer. Leacia would be proud of you if she knew.'

'She would not be proud of us, I think, for the way we treated you on the raft.'

'No, she would not. But here is a new beginning. The Great Whale is dead but his love for us lives on in my heart. He loved you despite your generation being the cause of his untimely death. He was a great lover of the world. You have cared for me and brought me back from death. It is Her Spirit's will. It could not be otherwise.'

'Oh, Indra. I am so glad you are here with us.' She leaned forward and they hugged.

Again Gerda leaned forward and they hugged.

'What is it, Gerda? You are troubled.'

'The males brought some fermented drink to the fire this evening. Everyone drank it. I had some too. Suyra drank a lot. She was the first one to drink and it changed her, Indra.'

'How changed?'

'She lay down with Jesson on the rocks. I think they will be bonded tonight without ceremony. I do not know what happened — I left the camp.'

'Perhaps we cannot expect such ceremony in this new land, Gerda.'We have to adjust. We are all in Her hands. I am hungry, have you brought me something to eat?'

'Here.' said Gerda, handing her the cold hunk of whale meat. 'I am sorry it is cold but it has been dried. It is too late to light a fire here tonight.'

'Why are they camping away from here, Gerda?' Indra asked, as she bit into the whale meat.

'Are they exploring?'

'We have found fire in the rock,' replied Gerda. 'It just spits and burns and needs no wood. Suyra says it is a gift from Her Spirit's heart, it is a miracle. They have made camp around it tonight. We took water from the geyser as there is no fresh water there.'

'Her Spirit is bountiful to have provided fresh water also.'

'The water is warm and tastes strange but we all drink it. It was the first thing we saw as we approached the new land after the storm. A great spurt of steaming water, nearly as tall as a tree. We made our way towards it. You will see it tomorrow — it is quite a sight.'

'Water as tall as a tree does sound intriguing. What about food? I can see you are not growing hungry. What is this I am eating? I have tasted something like it long ago, but I do not remember what...'

'Oh, Indra.' Gerda dropped her gaze. She felt suddenly frightened and disturbed in the presence of the older woman. The shaman who had called the whale.

'What is it?' Indra suddenly felt herself growing hot and panicky.

What was Gerda hiding? Then suddenly she knew.

'The whale… Am I eating whale meat?' she yelled with a burning anger. 'How could you dare!' she screamed, spitting the remains out of her mouth. And then, softly, seeing the shaking girl before her, she said, almost to herself, 'How could you know?'

There was silence for a few moments, then Gerda broke the silence, her eyes downcast: 'Do you want me to go?'

'No, Gerda, stay with me. You did what you thought was best and because of this I live, but I shall be very sad tonight, and cold. I shall need your warmth.'

Together they sat in silence, the candlelight flickered over the stone of the small chamber. Indra broke the silence at last. 'I loved him and he, in his whale way, loved me.'

Tears flowed softly over her cheeks as she rocked to and fro. A long loud wordless chant was wrung from the depths of her. Keening that echoed round the empty wasteland to be lost, drowned in the relentlessness of waves.

Shroud

In the early morning light Indra sat watching the natural warm fountain that spurted strongly from the depths of this young land.

She felt an especial alertness, a sharpening of the senses that reminded her of childhood. The splashing of water on the new-formed rocks, the gurgling of the stream, the backdrop sound of sea-breathing, formed a new synthesis of resonance that revived her.

Indra breathed deeply, inhaling the strange, new air, then exhaling breathily the bad airs of her recent fever.

Gerda lay sleeping in the shallow rock, tired out by the night of emotion they had shared. Indra walked towards the sea in measured steps taking in the desolate colourless landscape of rocks and boulders. The tattered, jagged wreck of the theatre raft lay at a tilted angle just above the shoreline. Some brightly coloured silk hangings fluttered sadly, like party guests who cannot find their party and have ended up in the wrong place.

Indra thought of the wonderful feast dances she had taken part in on that theatre raft. She remembered the sea of cheering faces, or the even greater acclaim when the audience spontaneously got to their feet and walked slowly down the ramps, humming, to surround the performers. Then the performers would sit back-to-back in a circle while the entire audience hummed together, sometimes getting louder and more intense — changing notes from high to low to become a three-dimensional sound mosaic that deeply acknowledged the performers gifts and uplifted them as much as the audience had been uplifted by their art.

Sometimes this auditory appreciation was as long as the previous performance, then the voices would die away and the peace would be kept before the greetings. Such wonderful quintessential moments would never again recur on this theatre raft, thought Indra sadly. It looked totally beyond repair. She knew then that they were completely stranded.

How she longed for her bobbing raft beneath her feet. The stillness of this land seemed unnatural, for she no longer felt the rocking sensation of living on the sea. This time, however, she felt no fear and had no sensation of the land dropping away.

Feeling disinclined to mount the boards she walked on past the theatre raft. The rocks on the shoreline were taking on a green-grey hue and, on closer examination, Indra saw that lichens were growing on the rocks. A host of little crabs scuttled in and out of rock-pools, hiding under the clumps of seaweed that had attached itself here and there to the rocks. White birds wheeled above the foam and smaller scuttling birds watched the sea intently from their rocky vantage point, sometimes unexpectedly flopping into the water to forage below the surface. Indra felt she was not yet ready to follow their example.

She debated with herself the merits of an early morning swim in unknown waters on her first, fully conscious morning in this new environment. Even though her spirit was crying out for the motion of the waves, she decided to sit by a small rocky inlet, trailing her feet in the warm water. Later

Indra searched the shoreline for stranded shell fish to eat.

By the time she had eaten the sun was high in the sky and she felt decidedly stronger. She returned to the water tree fountain in order to assuage her thirst and check on Gerda. She found the young girl was still fast asleep.

Unable to be sensible any longer, Indra threw caution to the winds and followed the stream down to the inlet. She plunged into the clear, refreshing water that washed away all traces of her feverish days and nights. The matted hair, caked with blood was freed again to flow like the water she swam in. How she revelled in this freedom, her taut limbs became relaxed and lost their aching tiredness.

Nearing the shore Indra heard a barely discernible cry brought to her on the freshening breeze. She walked as fast as she was able back over the rocks towards the camp. The cry had held a note of fear and, as she passed the theatre raft, she picked up a small rigging spar. Just in case, she thought to herself.

When she reached the camp it still seemed completely deserted. She walked over to the rock chamber where she had left Gerda and found her there, clinging to the rocks beneath her, as though she had scant assurance of their permanence or stability. When Indra called to her from above, Gerda looked up briefly then screamed. Gerda was so frightened she barely recognised Indra and looking up at her had only served to heighten the sensation that she was falling forever into a bottomless pit.

Indra jumped down beside her. Totally disorientated by the speed of this move, Gerda hit her head on the rock. Regretting her fast action and cradling Gerda's bleeding head, Indra tried to prise Gerda's hand from the rock but Gerda only cried and moaned in abject terror. 'The new land,' she gasped. 'The new land is falling!'

For the next few hours Indra cared for Gerda as Aaron had cared for her in the mountain cave. How long ago it seemed, since she and Aaron had set off on their journey through the mountain. Indra tried to reassure Gerda that the new land was not falling, and that her fear would pass. Finally, after many hours of tension, mediated somewhat by Indra's constant caring massage, exhaustion took over and Gerda slept. Indra carefully wrapped her in the silks and emerged from the crevice. She felt very stiff and sore after so many hours in such a cramped position.

Looking westward, Indra saw a few pink clouds gathering towards sunset. Turning east she made out a dark figure hurrying towards the camp. As he got nearer Indra felt sure it was Jesson although she could not yet discern his features, but because she was a dancer-performer, she had an innate understanding and focus on the way people fill their space and Jesson had an air of authority unusual in a male.

Perhaps, thought Indra a little uneasily, this will be a feature of the new land, a change in the balance. The males will no longer need to depend on us to go to the Island for the provisioning. They too will become gatherers and providers if this new land flourishes.

Indra sat down on a rock feeling slightly dizzy herself at the enormity of the social consequences of this new order. Surely it was not possible that males should stand equal in Her sight. Was this what the Great Spirit, the life-giver, was leading them towards on the new land? Many males she had met had seemed spiritually inept. The deeper spirituality, the oneness with Her

Spirit, seemed to be a language few males could comprehend. Intuition and telepathy was lost on them.

There was no large temple raft on the male raft system. In fact they had no system, merely rafts chaotically rambling across the seas. It was their usefulness the males thought about most. Their life was spent preening themselves to heights of physical fitness to be ready for the feastings, to be chosen. Surely they desired only to be used in this way. And yet...

'Greetings of evening, Indra.' Jesson's resonant voice broke in on her musings.

'Greetings, Jesson. You look a mess.'

Jesson gazed down at his blood-stained clothes and hands. 'Sorry, Indra. I should have washed in the sea. I did not know you would be well. I am glad that it is so.'

He looked at her momentarily and then away. He was enjoying being admonished by this older woman and his excitement showed. How he would like her to feel moon passion. Again he looked at her briefly through lowered eyelids, wondering if she had read his thoughts — after all she was a great shaman. Suddenly he knew he was blushing. He turned back towards the way he had come in order to hide the heat in his face.

Males! thought Indra indulgently. After all we are virtually alone and they often long for an older women to take notice of them...

'I came for Gerda.' said Jesson. 'Our other camp is along the beach.'

'Yes, Gerda told me about the whale meat,' whispered Indra.

'Indra, I...' Jesson, covered in whale blood from head to foot, felt tongue tied and rather afraid. He had led the attack on the whale.

Had she forgiven him? Did she remember? What might this shaman woman do?

The closest he had ever come to feeling this way was when, as a tiny boy, his mother had left him for the first time, on the male rafts.

Then, as now, he had felt guilty and afraid and unable to express his feelings. After a few minutes Jesson looked at Indra briefly. 'I regret that we hurt you,' he said simply and knelt to kiss her hand.

He looked up at her, his eyes brimming with tears.

She too cried in the emotion of the moment. 'I forgive you,' she bent down and kissed his forehead. They were still for a moment, the white birds wheeling on the thermals hundreds of feet above them.

Looking up at Indra, Jesson asked, 'Where is Gerda? We need her at the fire-camp. Suyra has gone mad. She has fallen down close to the fire and will not get up. If we try to move her she screams and clings to the rock. She says that the land is falling.'

'Gerda has the sickness also. Can you carry her as far as the fire camp?'

'I can carry her as far as the fire camp, if I must.' replied Jesson, rather reluctantly.

'Do not fear, Jasse. The sickness will not pass from Gerda to you. I will talk to you all when we reach the fire camp. Hurry now and drink your fill of water. I will give Gerda some water then we shall start our journey. You must take me to the camp as quickly as possible. I do not know how much time we have left.'

Much affected by these words and the urgency of her voice, Jesson ran towards the stream, while Indra attended to Gerda. With great difficulty and much screaming on Gerda's part, they managed to lift her out of the hollow in the rock. Indra dropped back into the tiny chamber for Gerda's medicine bag, before the little party set off slowly across the rocky twilight shore.

Gerda proved an extremely difficult burden on their journey that evening. When she was coming out of a faint she would grab at Jesson and shift her weight, trying to regain her balance. Several times they fell together in a heap. Gerda's vertigo caused her to fall very heavily and the third time they fell Gerda struck her head and lost consciousness completely.

There was no sound at the fire camp when the party arrived. The first thing Indra was strongly aware of was the strange smell that hung about the camp. She identified the pervasive, metallic smell of blood and also a peculiar smell that Indra thought was somehow connected with the eerie fire that hissed and spat from the rock.

Another unfamiliar smell came from several hollowed-out gourds that Indra had never seen before.

'What is it, Jesson?' she asked, indicating a gourd.

'Grog,' he replied, putting it to his lips. 'I could do with some of that. I feel bruised from head to foot.'

'What is grog?' asked Indra, although she already knew the answer.

'Fermented drink, Indra. All us males drink it when we are searching on the high sea. Our generation women have been drinking it too. Would you like to try some? Will you drink with me, Indra? Then we could keep warm together somewhere.'

'No, Jesson. Take me to Suyra, she needs my help. Then sleep, for I will talk to you all in the morning.'

In the small hours of the night, Indra dozed fitfully beside Suyra.

As the dawn light streaked across the barren landscape Indra made her way over the rocks towards the swelling surf for a morning bathe to wash away the stinking sweat of fever which still clung about her.

The shoreline was dominated by the dark hulk of her beloved whale.

The stink emanating from the great carcass made her retch. She ran and jumped into the sea and ploughing through the swell she dived, surfacing only briefly before swimming on again. At last she could no longer smell the stench and then the tears came. The juxtaposition of the deep love and the revulsion vied within her and she knew that she must soon return to that forsaken shore. That those who were the very cause of her deep anguish needed her help and care.

Suddenly a cheerful face bobbed up beside her and a dolphin swam around her chattering.

'Twoclickslong!' cried Indra in joyful recognition of the dolphin that had returned her to the rafts.

Indra put out her arm and peacefully they lolled together as the sun rose higher in the sky. Indra felt comforted by the presence of the dolphin, the limitless energy of its being consoled and strengthened her. Suddenly energy surged within her like rivulets of light. She felt renewed, reborn in the knowledge of love and that this love within her belonged to all that were receptive to its flow. Indra looked into the dolphin's eye.

'Thank you,' she said, hugging him. Indra and the dolphin swam and laughed together. She knew that she could now face the dead thing on the beach — she now knew more of death and more of life.

Turning towards the distant shore, Indra saw a strange sight. The whale, it seemed, had grown completely white, as if a great surreal shroud had been thrown over the vast carcass. She resurfaced again nearer the whale and she realised with some irony that, although that which was beneath it was dead, the shroud lived.

As she reached the rocks to clamber out of the swell, disturbed by her presence, the shroud lifted and the great white birds flew silently away. Indra was left staring up at the tattered, bloody flanks. Turning away retching, she saw the dolphin's cheerful face quite close and, recovering herself a little, she waded out towards him again.

'I will need you again soon, my friend. Stay near these shores and listen for my call.' Indra turned inland and wondered whether the dolphin would wait for her, but in her present mood she had no doubt that a dolphin would surface when the time came. Nearing the camp, Indra heard someone screaming and broke into a run.

When she looked down at the fire camp from her vantage point on the high rock above the fire it seemed as if she was caught up in some outlandish nightmare. Three of the males clung to the rocks, writhing, and their screams echoed around the blood stained rocks. Everyone was covered in dried blood from the whale cutting. Those who were not rolling on the ground in abject terror were very frightened. They clung to each other in groups, seemingly unable to move, fearing the strange madness that was happening to the friends around them.

Indra called to Jesson and beckoned him. He climbed up to her while the others stared up at her clean, commanding form. 'Jesson, go to each group and tell them to follow me. We must talk urgently. We'll have to leave the screaming ones alone for a while. There is very little we can do for them anyway until I have talked to the rest of you. Tell them it is imperative that they come.'

Jesson took a step back and nearly slipped on the rock. An imperative was rarely invoked. Then he looked at the young people below him and realised that this was probably the only thing that would move them in their bemused state. 'I will bring them to you, Indra.'

Briefly he bowed his head, the male's mark of respect to the women of the council. In doing this he acknowledged the wisdom of her years and her sex. Usually collective decisions were made by the older women who oversaw the whole social system. Males' decisions, if any, were of lesser importance and carried little weight.

Indra led the demoralised band of young people towards the relative quiet of the sea which swelled and sucked but rarely a wave broke unless there was storm change. Indra found an outcrop of volcanic rock which gave her some height above the crowd and turned towards the sea for a few minutes.

When they were gathered about her, Indra turned slowly towards their upturned faces. 'You have brought me much anger,' she shouted.

Then, her voice became almost a whisper. 'You have brought me great pain.' She paused. They looked so shaken, so young.

'I know of the sickness and I know that I can help you and, if you should ask it of me, I shall stay a while with you. I will no longer look on your filth — I cannot bear your stench! Go to the sea and be cleansed and

return here by noon. There is much to do.'
Again she turned from them and gazed
seawards.

When they returned damp and silent from
the sea. She stood facing the land. She
watched them as they gathered before her.

'We will sit.' Without a word they sat, the
males with eyes downcast.

'You well know that I have no reason to
love you.' Indra began. 'But I have known of
love that transcends our present state. Love
that is whole and true. It has opened light
within me to now offer you my help. Do
you ask this of me?'

'We ask it,' replied the young women.

'Then I will stay with you a while. When
your need has lessened you will find that I
have gone. I will return to the Island and
send you help.'

In the stunned silence that followed this
statement, Indra watched their upturned
faces and felt safer. Had their despair
curdled into re-kindled anger, she could
again have become a victim of their
youthful excesses. She was protecting
herself with a cloak of mystery and power.
She could see by their expressions that they

were already regarding her as a shaman and indeed, she thought ruefully, perhaps that is a part of the truth. I do not feel for them the anger that is rightfully mine. I feel love — a love made greater somehow by what we have shared.

Aloud, she said. 'The Great Spirit is with us!'

Indra bowed her head slightly, her arms outstretched, palms facing the earth mother. The young people followed the well-known invocation. Then, as each felt the moment was right, they slowly turned the palms and their faces towards the sky and whispered.

'From stardust to stardust.'

Minutes later, when their attention was again upon her, Indra said, 'Now to practicalities. Each one of you will get the screaming sickness.' There was an audible intake of breath. Each of them had seen friends disorientated and clinging to rock in abject fear.

'But it will pass and none of you will return your dust to the Great Spirit because of it. I, myself, have passed through the great terror and I know it does not last. I will show you how to massage and reassure those who have been struck down. This will help to ease the pain of their terror.

Also, some of you must fetch sea water to wash the blood from those that are now afflicted. Then a large group of you must take the sail to bring more fresh water. If many of you get struck down together there will be no-one to fetch it, so we must have a good supply.'

'Some of you must go to the whale. When you bathed you have seen that the white birds are gathering. The whale is principally what you will live on until provisions come from our fertile Island. His whale flesh will sustain you. The whale gave himself to you...' Indra's voice faltered. 'And you must reap what is, to me, a bitter harvest. Offer none of it to me. I will eat whatever else you can find on this barren land.'

'There are white bird's eggs, Indra,' called Caley from the crowd.

'Thank you Caley, perhaps you will find some for me,' smiled Indra.

The others laughed gently. The egg hunt was a game for children on the rafts and Caley, though shy, was the tallest woman of that generation, towering above most of the males. Indra smiled, a sad smile.

'Decide amongst yourselves who will do what, but be as quick as you can. There is much to do, we do not have long before each one of you will be struck down.'

'Later I will tell you why this strange fear occurs and how you can help each other when it comes. I will not leave you until some of you are again well enough to take care of others. Gerda and Suyra will probably be amongst the first to recover as they were the first to be affected.'

Their upturned faces looked concerned. Looking back a few minutes later, Indra saw the group was already dispersing. She walked slowly inland and, beneath her hand that rested, momentarily, on the volcanic rock, she felt something unexpectedly soft. Looking down she saw two tiny blades of grass growing in a crevice of the rock and across part of this little hollow a web was stretched. Borne on southerly winds, these were among the first migrants of the new land. Smiling to herself at this confirmation of new life, Indra continued on her way.

Out Crossing

In the early dawn light Indra stood in the shadows silently calling the dolphin to her. Presently a laughing head emerged from the waves a few yards away. Indra waded towards the young dolphin, speaking softly. 'We have a long way to go, my friend. I wish to return to the Island.'

When she reached the dolphin he allowed her to put her arms around him resting her head against his, she again repeated her request, trying to send an image of the Island telepathically. He nodded and chattered and she received an image of the undersides of the raft system on which she had lived.

'Yes,' she whispered. 'Twoclickslong that is where I want to go. Will you take me there?'

The dolphin reared back, breaking her grasp with his euphoric energy, rearing out of the water as he careered back at a furious speed he chattered at her. Then, like a clown, he flopped right over on his back with a great splash and disappeared from view. For a moment Indra wondered whether she had lost him. Had her request been too much for him? She knew, with the certainty of the image she had received, that he had understood her.

Then, between her legs, came the familiar persistent nudging of the dolphin's bulbous nose. Indra grasped the fin and the next moment they were careering through the waves, soon leaving the new land far behind.

It was an exhilarating journey through sunshine and water but after a few hours Indra rolled off the dolphin's back, completely exhausted. She floated on the swell of the sea, wondering if she would again see her beloved raft system.

It had taken them many days journey, by raft, to cover the distance between the two lands. She realised she had been as impetuous as the youngsters she had left behind in undertaking such a long sea journey without forethought. Sometimes, Indra, she mused to herself, you are dangerously impractical. The dolphin swam around her recumbent body, its energy seemingly inexhaustible. Indra's arms ached and she felt dispirited and alone. Suddenly she realised she was completely alone. She looked around at the endless horizon with a stab of fear. No formal communication had taken place between herself and the dolphin — had the dolphin left her forever to sink through the waters to the Great Spirit, her mother? For a long moment Indra prayed. Then the words of the Great Whale came back to her and she knew she had a destiny to fulfil, a destiny that did not lie between the two lands — but linked them.

More relaxed, Indra lay on her back gazing up at the clouds — the white sky-rafts of childhood myths and legends. The dolphin surfaced beside her and in its mouth were some fronds of reddish weed. Gently, very gently, he put some tendrils into her mouth. She sucked them, then nibbled them. Strangely, they did not taste salty. They seemed to be juicy, fresh water plants. She ate some more and began to feel revitalised.

Indra sent a telepathic question to the dolphin and received a strange image of broiling water coming from a rock fissure on which the weed grew. She concluded that this swirling water from the rocks was a fresh water geyser like the one on the new land. Whatever the truth of it, she knew this fleshy weed would enable her to resume her long journey. With renewed energy she took the rest of the plant from the dolphin and slung it over her shoulders like a great red mantle. Feeling a nudging between her legs Indra grabbed the dolphin and together they resumed their journey southwards.

*   *   *

Indra was exhausted by the days and nights of travelling with the dolphin. At night she had lolled on his back bathed in starlight that was beautiful and cold. Again and again she woke screaming with fear, having dreamed of she was again on the theatre raft, seeing the mast being rammed into the whales flesh.

During the day she sucked the fleshy seaweed and longed for rest. She was riding high on the dolphin's back when at last she saw the dark masts of the raft system as the sun began to set. They will be amazed to see me after all this time, she thought. What a homecoming it will be. There are so many rafts — perhaps it is feast time. Mione, my dearest daughter, it will be so good to hold you in my arms.

Suddenly she felt the dolphin's muscles tighten and he picked up speed. Indra looked about and saw the reason for the dolphin's strange behaviour. Only a short distance away a dark fin sped through the water. A shark was cutting through the waves towards them. Indra bent low on the dolphin's back. The spray stung her face so great was their acceleration. What is attracting it? she thought wildly. Sharks don't usually attack for no reason.

Then a gravelly spasm of pain gnawed its way across her stomach and she knew only too well what had attracted her predator. Moon-time flow, a portion of her life's blood, her Gift to the Great Spirit, which the males emulated in their blood brother dance was what had caused such deadly interest.

With frightening speed the dolphin careered through the waves towards the raft system. We're going to crash, thought Indra. If the shark doesn't get me first. Then, with a giant surging leap, the dolphin rose up out of the water with its human cargo, twisted in mid-air and returned to the sea. Indra, her tenacious grip loosened by the dolphin's unexpected virtuosity, screamed as she was flung through the air onto the rough boards of the raft system.

Return

Painfully Indra got up and rubbed her bruised left hip. Her left shoulder was bleeding slightly as she walked slowly over the boards to rest herself against the hut wall. Trying to get her bearings Indra gazed across the maze of rafts. She had hoped to call to someone nearby but this was an unpopulated part of the raft system.

Peering in at the hut window she saw stacks of paintings and highly decorated musical instruments. Looking at the next few rafts Indra realised, by their undecorated nature, that this was a storage area. Disappointed that no-one seemed to have seen her spectacular arrival and rather disheartened by the lack of any sort of welcome, Indra walked towards the centre of the raft system which seemed to be deserted. Where was everyone? Why were there no shouts of children playing?

As she neared the inhabited rafts she heard a low humming which explained why no-one was about — it was communion. The

137

time when every woman and child held communion with the Great Spirit. Indra smiled, had she forgotten so much? Her time of giving blood usually coincided with this ritual every month and, if the males were gathering, they too would emulate the women's communion with the Great Spirit.

The last trails of sunset lit the western horizon, a slight breeze blew and it was growing dark. Indra began to feel very cold, standing at a hut door in her damp silk under-shawls. She stood outside the hut shivering, she could not disturb the deep concentration of the communion.

After a few minutes of inaction, Indra could bear it no longer. She pushed open the door and stepped into the dark interior. She was overwhelmed by the familiar scents around her. She had missed them so much, that emotion overtook her and for a few moments she could not speak. The humming stopped and the little shrine lamp was immediately relit. Then a woman turned to close the door and saw Indra.

She cried out softly and stood stock still, trembling a little. Indra saw at once that this woman was not on of the present women's council. She could also see that this woman was frightened of her.

'What is it? Whispered Indra in hushed tones. 'Why are you frightened? I am Indra, I have been away. I need to dry myself and I need some dry shawls — and a special silk for the Gift. What is your name?'

'My name is Nyiam. Indra, is it really you? We thought you had returned to the Great Spirit. I will help you to get dry. Indra! You look so wild!'

Indra smiled to herself. Wild! I probably do look wild after such a journey!

To Nyiam she said simply 'Thank you.' She did not know what else to say.

Nyiam opened a chest and handed Indra an un-dyed rough silk with which to dry herself. She reached under the bed and, with shaking hands, she undid a silk roll of carefully folded silk shawls.

'Choose any of these, Indra. Please regard this hut as your own. Use any of my creams and brushes. I will light another lamp for you. Would you like some tea?' Nyiam reached into the grass-filled box for the warm kettle.

'Thank you, Nyiam, that would be wonderful. It has been so long since I drank tea. I would like some honey if you have some.'

Indra finished drying and rubbed some healing cream into her bruised hip and shoulder. Then, tying several shawls around her body and one around her head for warmth, Indra settled herself beside the grass box with the warm tea that Nyiam had given her. Nyiam began to relax, Indra looked far less strange now that her snow-white, windswept hair was hidden from view. Some of the elders went grey in old age but white hair on such a young woman was startling and there was something disturbingly untamed about Indra — something unpredictable.

Nyiam wanted to get away from her, to be with familiar women. Indra seemed to have brought something of the outside in with her. She had been off the rafts too long. She was no longer a raft woman.

Indra was unaware of her disturbing appearance but she knew that this woman, whose hospitality she had sought, was treating her with awesome respect.

'Shall I get someone? Someone should be told that you are here.'

'Everyone will be getting ready to sleep now but Leacia might be on watch. Could you wake my daughter, Mione of the Moon Generation. I wish her to know tonight that I have not yet returned to the Great Spirit.'

With a sense of relief Nyiam reached down and took Indra's hand.

'I will return soon with your daughter. I will send Leacia to you if she is on watch.'

Indra sipped her delicious tea and listened to the sounds around the hut, the sucking and splashing of the wavelets gently slapping the logs beneath her, the cacophony of creaking logs, the occasional far off cry of a baby or young child. How good it was to hear these familiar sounds. Indra hugged herself with joy at the sheer comfort these sounds gave her. She looked around at Nyiam's hut. The large bed had a beautifully embroidered silk coverlet, the silks covering the walls were very old and had been carefully mended and handed down through many generations. They told of the old stories of life on the rafts and the myths and legends surrounding the Island. One particularly ancient silk hanging caught Indra's attention. Although the silk colours had long faded into obscurity, the stitched outlines were still visible. It showed the Island with the great mountain outlined by a motif of the sun and below the Island, apparently holding the Island on its back, was the outline of the Great Whale.

Indra recalled then the legend she had been told as a child, that the Island was held up above the sea by the leviathan. It seemed like a message to her, this ancient silk was a talisman, a part of growing her own interior mountain, a way to express a part of her recent experience.

This legend had never been danced before, certainly not in her living memory.

It was at this point that Indra crystallised her plan of action. In her mind's eye she could see herself in the Sacred Cave dancing — expressing her story through movement and music and later weaving a silk hanging on a large loom. As she wove she would tell the story of the legend pictured in Aaron's cave and her recent experience. She would call for a meeting of the women's council in ritual clothing — time then for decisions to be made.

Indra was deep in her reverie when the door opened. Mione came in and quietly closed the door. For a few moments she watched her mother whom she thought, at first was asleep. Then Indra opened her eyes and looked towards her tall daughter. Emotion ran too deep for words. Indra rose from her chair and Mione leapt across the room and flung her arms around her mother. Indra rested her head on Mione's breast, then looked up and took Mione's face between her shaking hands as they kissed. It was almost as if the roles were reversed. Mione had blossomed into full womanhood during the time Indra had been away. Indra, always small boned and delicate. She had grown more thin and fragile, yet a great strength and vitality fuelled an inner light which gave her a wild ethereal quality of a delicate moonlit flower being blown in a strong wind.

Finally Indra sat down, still holding Mione's hands. Mione sat at her feet and Indra spoke, gazing lovingly at her daughter.

'You have grown, my daughter.'

They both laughed, acknowledging the truth of this remark.

'Indra, my mother, you too are greatly changed.'

'A sea change,' replied Indra, smiling.

'Indeed,' laughed Mione. 'Nyiam says your hair is white — can I see it?'

'White?' questioned Indra. 'I did not know my hair had grown white.'

'I understand now why she shook when she first saw me. I must have looked strange when I first appeared. When I go next to the Island I shall look into the clear pool and give myself a shock! Here take off the turban and see for yourself.'

Indra leaned forward and Mione carefully unwound the cloth. Indra's hair was as white as the snows of Arrat. When she flicked it back it stuck out in all directions around her face. Mione could not prevent a look of horror passing over her face. What a wild, strange creature her mother looked with her small frame, her child-like face with strange frizzy white hair.

'You don't like it Mione, I can see that.' Indra caught a strand of her hair and examined it closely. 'It's certainly unusual, unheard of for a woman of my age. I wonder when it happened? I'm sorry it has shocked you — it has certainly shocked me. I did not know myself until this moment. Shall we borrow Nyiam's combs and see if we can improve things?'

'Yes mother,' smiled Mione. 'I will try to comb it and plait it. It will take a long time to do, it looks very tangled.'

'Well, it has not been combed for a very long time. How long have I been away?'

'About one moon I think.' Mione gently combed her mother's long hair, starting at the edges.

'Only one moon…. yes, it can only be one. It seems to me that I have been away a great deal longer than that.'

'You look as if you have been far away, Indra, my mother.'

'Yes, very far, my daughter. I have much to tell you. I have decided on a way in which I wish to tell the strange story of my journey. It is important to the future of us all and it must be told in a special way. Now that the theatre raft is gone we will have to gather in the Sacred Cave. That would be the perfect venue for what I have in mind. I'm sure the women's council will agree… Mione, why have you stopped combing my hair?'

'You know? You know about the theatre raft?'

'Yes, Mione. And I know about the Cloud Generation that has been lost to our people.'

'Mother, how can you know of these things? You have been lost to us for a month — since before the great wave. Did Nyiam tell you of it?'

'No. No, Mione. Carry on combing, try one of Nyiam's brushes now. That's better. Tell me about this wave.'

'A wall of water flooded the Island. We sheltered in the far lagoon so our rafts suffered little damage.'

Indra was suddenly aware that she was very hungry. She leaned forward and reached into the box beside her and uncovered several small warm loaves. 'I must eat, Mione. Can you get me one of Nyiam's plates. Where has she got to? Isn't she coming back tonight?'

'No, she is staying with her sister. She says we can use her hut for as long as we wish. She will not return until we have gone.' Mione handed her mother a plate and smiled.

'Is she frightened of me?' asked Indra.

'Yes, a little. You are so changed.'

'Do you think others will feel the same way?' asked Indra, tearing off a piece of fresh baked bread.

'I think so,' replied Mione.

'Do you feel frightened of me?' said Indra, biting into the rich crust.

'There is something that sets you apart from us, others will see it, but no, I am not frightened. I thought that you had given yourself to the Great Spirit and now the Great Spirit has given you back to me.' Mione tore off a piece of bread for herself. 'I'll make some tea.'

After making the tea, Mione resumed combing and brushing Indra's wild hair. Even when it was completely tangle-free it still stuck out like a halo around Indra's head. Mione suggested that she should braid it, but Indra knew that it would be uncomfortable for her to sleep with it tied.

'Leave it, Mione. I will wrap it in a turban tomorrow, perhaps. I know it looks strange but that may be an advantage. I have many things to organise tomorrow. Let us sleep soon. Stay with me Mione, I need your warmth.'

Indra slipped the shawls off her shoulders, leaving only the white silk under-shawl.

The raft women wore un-sewn silk tied or tucked around themselves and put all their energies in the making of their clothing and into the weaving and dying processes. Sewing was only used in the stitching of pictorial wall hangings which they appliquéd, and in the making of the silk sails. The males often embroidered their exaggerated loin pouches in order to draw attention to their usefulness at feast times when they paraded their bronzed, oiled bodies before the women.

Indeed, the male pouches were intricately sewn and the women had not time or inclination for sewing clothes which was deemed a male pursuit.

The soft feather bed felt wonderful to Indra's tired and aching limbs. Mione brought a little oil lamp over to the shelf beside the bed. 'Let me massage you, Indra. It will relax you before you sleep.'

Mione started lifting the tops off the little jars that lined the shelf. Some jars were very ancient and had been passed down through generations of women. Some jars were empty. Mione picked up a little green container and smelled its contents, 'This smells good, my mother.' She passed the jar to Indra.

'Perfect,' pronounced Indra with a sigh. Mione started massaging Indra's feet. Indra could feel waves of tension rolling off her.

When she had given her mother an all-over body massage, Mione cradled Indra's head in her lap and gave Indra a gentle neck and facial massage. Rhythmically smoothing her mother's forehead Mione softly chanted the ancient song of welcome. Finally, she bent down and kissed her mother's forehead then, blowing out the light, she rolled under the coverlet.

Indra kissed her daughter's cheek. 'Thank you Mione. It is good to be home. Drift gently in dream time.'

* * *

Indra awoke early. In the eastern sky a pearly lightness heralded the new day. Taking off her under-shawl she carefully folder the special silk for the Gift which she would replace with a fresh one after her swim. Indra slipped into the sea-lane between Nyiam's raft and the agri-rafts. She swam around the corner of the adjacent agri-raft towards the open sea and, after relieving herself well beyond the raft system, she swam back to Nyiam's raft. Indra dried herself with the white shawl that she had discarded, rinsed the red Gift silk and entered the hut. She undid the small roll of under-shawls and tied the top one around her body. In choosing from the larger bale of coloured shawls she took more care, finally deciding on a pair of pale shimmering shawls to borrow from Nyiam.

When she was fully dressed Indra woke her sleeping daughter. 'Come with me Mione. I want to have breakfast early. There is much I have to do.'

Indra brushed her hair while Mione went for a quick swim. When she returned to Indra again asked her to hurry.

'I hope you won't be upset, Mione, if I do not wrap my hair.'

'Indra, my mother,' said Mione, looking at her mother whilst she tied her outer shawls, 'I know you have your reasons... but...' she giggled. 'You do look strange!'

'I know,' smiled Indra. 'I think it must have been the shark! Come on, we must break our fast early.'

'Shark mother! What are you telling me?'

The sky was quite light now and a few small golden clouds hid the full heat of the sunrise. There was very little movement as yet on the rafts, but as they crossed the link bridge to the eating rafts Leacia called out to them as she was swimming in from the open sea.

'Mione. Mione, wait... Who...? Indra! My goodness, your hair! We thought that you had gone to the Great Spirit. It looks as though you almost did!'

'That is true, Leacia!' called back Indra smiling. 'Several times the Great Spirit stood near to me with her arms outstretched, but she did not kiss me and so I have returned to you.'

Leacia swam under the link bridge on which they stood.

'I will join you shortly.'

'If we finish here before you arrive I shall be going to the Inner Sanctum. Please meet me there It is imperative that I talk to the council this morning.'

Leacia waved and nodded then, turning, she swam swiftly up the channel between the rafts.

Indra stood at the edge of the eating raft gazing at the Island while Mione got their breakfast. Only the old cook was up this early in the morning. She stared at Indra as she gave Mione the breakfast.

In the bright morning air half a dozen little children came running, breathlessly, over a link bridge to get their collecting baskets.

Several of them were carrying eggs and flying fish. When they saw Indra they all stopped silently and stared. One tiny boy-child dropped his egg in surprise and started crying. His sister gathered him up and, grabbing the nearest baskets, they all fled across the nearest link bridge.

'An interesting reaction!' commented Indra as they sat down. 'Now, Mione, after breakfast I want you to gather all the dancers, mimers, artists and musicians. Anyone of the company that wishes to work with me must be prepared for three days of very intensive and unusual work before the performance. This will be a new and epic production.'

'I will talk to everyone when we are gathered together. We will meet in the sight of the Great Spirit when the sun is at its height. Before that I must talk to the women's council but I hope it will all be arranged by that time.

The Eye of Wisdom

Indra sat alone on the edge of the Eye of Wisdom — a vast dish that was set into the floor of the Inner Sanctum in the temple of the Great Spirit. The floor of this part of the temple was completely inlaid with mother of pearl. Where the floor dipped into the great shallow bowl, the patterning became almost mesmeric in its intensity and richness. The morning sunlight was muted by the plain white silks adorning the walls and ceiling, which added to the atmosphere of quiet splendour. With the doors open these long silk hangings rippled gently in the breeze. This place of contemplation was frequented mainly by the members of the council either singly or in full council. If a raft woman felt that she should become one of the council she would visit this inner sanctum alone and it was tradition among the raft women that when she emerged from the Eye of Wisdom, she would know if she had been truly called.

Indra listened to the strange, almost eerie, sound that pervaded the room. A soft booming resonance, as if a giant took breath, it was the rhythm of the sea swirling around the underside of the bowl-shaped floor. She looked up at the long silk thread hanging from the ceiling that held the Great Spirit's teardrop, poised and shimmering. A small shining tear that would occasionally drop, relatively loudly, into the bowl of wisdom.

If the tear ever fell into the bowl during a full council meeting it was thought to be a sign of great portent that signified the Great Spirit's intervention. It was believed that if the discussion saddened the Great Spirit Her tear would fall and the council would have to rethink the matter. In any event a tear drop at a full meeting was an extremely infrequent occurrence.

Indra was dressed in her full ceremonial robes and make up, only her white hair remained unadorned. She had been pleased to find her place in the robing room had been left undisturbed. As she sat in the inner sanctum waiting for the council to assemble, Indra practiced sending her energy across the Eye. Today, tired though she was, she would need to be exceptionally alert and extraordinarily persuasive in order to carry the council with her. Now it had begun, the rolling of the wave, and for a moment Indra held this thought and felt an acute sense of panic.

'Stage fright,' she smiled to herself. 'The Great Spirit is with me.'

The great curtain was pulled back and the women's council, an impressive sight in their full regalia, now filed silently into the room.

Indra stood up in respect of their arrival. Leacia led the procession of women around the bowl of wisdom. The last of the women came through and the curtain was pulled across. Everyone standing on the edge of the bowl stared at Indra in a shocked silence, for although they knew that she was back and that her hair was white, the actual reality of her being, held an enigmatic power that spoke of something outside their experience.

Indra made eye contact with each member of the council around the bowl as the last women closed the circle. They held hands and simultaneously they looked into the eye of wisdom and began a soft low vocal harmony, fusing their energies into the bowl, gradually climbing the harmonic scale. When one of the women eventually reached the highest note in the vocal range, she lifted her eyes towards the Great Spirit's tear. Every woman in the room knew that the consciousness had changed. One by one their harmonies died away and they looked up at the glistening tear until silence was reached, after which, within a few moments, they settled themselves cross-legged around the great bowl of wisdom in order to begin their council meeting.

Leacia was the first to speak. 'Greetings Indra, we are glad to see your safe return. I know that you have much to tell us but I wonder at you calling a meeting at this early hour on the very morning of your return.'

Indra took a deep breath.

'There is much urgency in what I have to do and you are right, Leacia, I have a great deal to tell you all. But I feel I must relate my story, at first, through dance and mime and music,'

'We have no theatre raft, Indra. It disappeared when the Cloud Generation left us,' replied Leacia. She had been somewhat surprised by Indra's answer to her greeting.

'The theatre raft and Cloud Generation are within my story,' said Indra.

Several of the women gasped.

'Then you know what happened to them?' asked Leacia.

'Yes,' said Indra quietly. 'I know.'

'Then you must tell us at once. We have been waiting for news of them.' Nibinie called angrily.

'The time is not right for me to tell you now. The way I tell my story could affect our entire future, The Cloud Generation is safe. I cannot tell you more than this,'

'But this is an outrage, Indra. You cannot keep this information to yourself. Why have the Cloud Generation not returned? Why have so few of the male rafts returned?'

'I know nothing certain about why many of the males have not returned but I do know where the young people are. But it is imperative that I tell my story as a whole. It is important to our whole future. What I am about to ask is, perhaps, unusual but you may be sure that I have the strongest reasons for asking this.'

'Ask it,' sighed Leacia. She was completely taken aback by her friend's assertive tone.

Her wildness, though muted by ceremonial dress, was as disconcerting as her manner.

'The Sacred Cave is the only place large enough to hold the entire population of our rafts.' Indra looked around the Eye, their adherence to the old ways was going to be difficult to break. 'Even if the theatre raft was here I have special reasons for wishing to use the Sacred Cave.'

'I know that traditionally children have never set foot on the Island, however I know of an older history where that tradition did not exist. We could leave the youngest children with the males that have returned, but as what happens now will affect all future generations, I know that it is important for the children to see this legend unfold and to help us decide what shall be done.'

'You speak in riddles, Indra. The women's council always make decisions for the raft people.'

'Perhaps, when I have told my story, the people will feel that we should decide for them. What I have to impart must be unfolded slowly in a special way. I just need three days to rehearse, then one day for the performance, one day for the telling of my story and one day for a discussion of the whole matter, and then...' Indra looked around the circle of women with an ironic half-smile on her face.

'...and then I shall have a day of rest!'

There was some laughter around the circle at this, but some of the older women still looked grim faced. Never before had the entire population of the raft system landed on the island together. Never before had the Sacred Cave been used in this way.

'No Indra!' called Oida. The old one had a low gravelly voice. 'We cannot allow this! We all know you and your imaginative ideas. It is just not practical. You cannot use our Sacred Cave for six days in this manner — it would be sacrilege.'

The majority of women around the circle nodded their heads and there was a general tone of agreement. Negative comments passed around the eye.

Indra was going too far. How dare she think of using the Sacred Cave for such an enterprise? When the uproar died down Oida spoke out. 'In the Great Spirit's name — no!'

Suddenly the Great Spirit's tear dropped loudly into the bowl of the Eye of Wisdom. For a few moments there was a stunned silence, then Indra spoke.

'The Great Spirit has made herself clear. It is the Great Spirit's will that we go to the Island. The musicians and dancers will be gathering outside. We will take a few rafts into the lagoon close to the Sacred Cave. Please be with me. It is imperative you are with me. Peace be with you.'

Indra stood up extending her arms as if to embrace the entire circle.

After a long moment of contemplation Leacia got up in one graceful movement and held her arms wide. One by one the entire council stood with arms gently extended around the bowl, except for Oida. Finally, with a sigh of resignation, she too, stood up stiffly and took part in the sign of trust in which they all leaned backwards, holding hands, their long hair brushing the shining inlaid floor. So far back did they bend that, had the trust been broken, they would all have fallen. This equilibrium was maintained while they intoned the litany. During the silence that followed every woman gradually pulled in her elbows until she was again standing upright. Indra looked round the circle.

'Thank you,' she spoke softly and then, with some reverence, she looked up at the Great Spirit's tear. 'Thank you,' she whispered.

Telling

During the next three days Indra and her company of dancers musicians and mimers worked tirelessly to reproduce Indra's story in its unspoken form. Indra had decided that certain sections of the work would be quite literal and other sections, such as her interaction with the whale, she would dance-conduct. Indra felt that the impact of her adventures would be too great if told without subtlety. Her people's lives had changed very little in the last few centuries. The formation of the new land, which was as yet unknown to them and the implications of it on their feminine society, would be shock enough. The historical background to their society, lost in the mists of time, needed to be brought to light if they were to make sense of their future existence. Indra's idea was that she should give the audience a taste of the truth through music, mime and dance before she changed their lives forever by revealing the living legend that had taken place.

The raft women were very creative and often quite lateral in their thinking and this meant there were few barriers between the arts. A great dancer would also strive to be a great musician — indeed as often as a composer wrote her music with a dance in mind, a dancer would choreograph a dance to which the musician would add her music.

A conductor would lead her orchestra by dancing her interpretation of the music. In this way old and familiar pieces of music could be rendered almost unrecognisable by the new dance of a conductor.

Musicians would often choreograph their own dance movements as they played, adding to the general interpretation of the piece. In fact, this was how Indra avoided directly telling her company the actuality of what had occurred. She used mime, dance and music to tell her story and left the company to interpret and extrapolate the full meaning of their work. It would have been inappropriate and counterproductive for the council to feel that the company had known the full extent of the story before they did.

At first the performance company were overawed by this woman that was known to them, and yet unknown. By the second day no-one was in any doubt but that the interpretation of this living legend was to be the climax of their artistic achievements. For although they did not understand it fully they could feel the depth of sorrow, of hope and above all, love that Indra embodied. There was an enigmatic vitality about her which flowed from her inspiring the company to new heights of performance.

On the morning of the third day everyone awoke with the dawn. The lagoon below the Sacred Cave rang with the shouts and laughter of the early morning swimmers. Soon dry, the women took a little time to brush each other's hair before breakfasting on dried fish and eggs which were brought each day from the raft city anchored close to the lagoon. As they waded through the shallows to the shore they chatted excitedly. Indra and Mione sat on their raft staring out to sea.

'Aren't you going up to the Sacred Cave this morning, Indra my mother?' asked Mione.

'To tell you the truth, Mione, I think I need to rest a while this morning if I am to be ready for tomorrow, and perhaps the company need some time without me. The only thing that we must do when I join them is to run through the entire sequence from beginning to end. Tell them I will be with them in a few hours. They can rehearse by themselves meanwhile.'

'Can I get you anything before I go?' asked Mione.

'Please put my brush and paints beside me, just in case something further occurs to me as I am resting.'

'Are you including the feast dance you were devising before you left?'

'Oh, Mione, I had forgotten. That is precisely where it should begin. Tell the dancers and musicians to be ready to add an extra sequence. Could you get that leaf from the top of my writing chest as well?'

Mione busied herself getting the things and setting them carefully beside Indra. Mione squatted down and kissed her mother and for a few moments smoothed her mother's brow. 'Rest a little, won't you?' said Mione as she stood up.

'I will rest, my daughter. Tell them I will be at the Sacred Cave at midday.'

'I will tell them mother,' smiled Mione, looking down at the small fragile looking lady whose head was surrounded by a halo of white hair.

*   *   *

As the sun began to set the women and children from the raft city gathered slowly on the shore of the lagoon below the sacred cave.

There was great excitement and not a little nervousness displayed by the young girls and children as they set foot on the Island for the first time. Some of them ran up the beach to play amongst the trees and watch the extraordinary display of multicoloured butterflies that danced around the exotic heat-sodden flowers. A family of pandas that had been stolidly munching bamboo shoots a short distance from the shoreline lumbered off to loose themselves in the camouflage of foliage. Drunken bees droned heavily, occasionally snapped from existence by bejewelled birds. Other young girls stayed close to their mothers, overawed by the new experience, some squatted down and made patterns in the sand with their fingers.

When the last of the women and children had reached the shore the women's council emerged in their full ceremonial regalia and boarded the long raft. They looked a formidable sight in their brightly coloured robes, with their many layers of silk, each layer was a different colour. From bright coral to the palest pink undergarment. Other colour layerings were from eggshell blue to blue of night. The slight breeze drew these veils apart showing the costumes to full advantage as the council punted slowly and solemnly towards the shore.

As they walked through the crowd they greeted special friends, sometimes squatting down occasionally to greet a child. Even though they were set apart from the other women by their special robes and duties, there was no real hierarchy amongst the women. The council of women was a well-loved tradition, the focal point of feasts. Any woman who felt the Great Spirit had called her could, at her own will, belong to the council.

The council slowly approached the path that led up to the Sacred Cave and the others fell in behind them. The low murmur of voices mingled with the suck and gentle thrust of the waves on the shore. There was an excited air of anticipation among the crowd. Never before had the whole raft city been vacated in this way. Only the few male rafts, clinging to the fringes of the raft city, showed any sign of movement.

Some of the males stood watching the great crowd of women and children slowly mounting the narrow path. They felt uneasy about being so close to the Island. None of them, or their forefathers, had set foot on the Island. They felt disquiet whenever they came close to it. Great and perilous journeys on the high seas held no fear for them, but this close to the Island — they felt a pervasive sense of dread.

The woman's island, as the males called it, held both fear and pleasure. They had to come to the women so their rafts could be provisioned in order for them to carry out their quest for new land. During the feast times they preened and strutted proudly before the women to gain attention and the sexual favours they craved after their long sea journeys. Some males deemed themselves artists and musicians, emulating the woman's creativity but they compartmentalised their skills. A male musician would only play one instrument. One who deemed himself a painter would concentrate on painting pictures and would not concern himself with other arts.

The raft women, in contrast to this, were fluidly creative and saw the interconnection between all art forms. Their beautifully decorated huts housed generations of artwork in many varied forms. When a raft woman could no longer dance, in great old age, she would begin her time of wisdom, her journey of return towards the Great Spirit.

*   *   *

In the darkness of the cave as they entered, the women and children saw a large circle of oil lamps. As their eyes got more accustomed to the shadowy light of the cave they could see mats had been placed on the rocks around this circle, tier upon tier as the rocky shelves formed a rough, but natural, amphitheatre. Only the final rock shelves were left unadorned by the lavishly embroidered mats. Some mats were generations old.

The upper reaches of the cave were covered in rock paintings. Here, too, oil lamps had been placed to illuminate the vast number of murals that rose to the rocky ceiling of the chamber. Some small lamps were floating in the reflective water, caught in a lip of rock, that dripped into a tiny shallow lake to one side of the cave. Never had the Sacred Cave looked more beautiful. The air of excitement stilled to an almost silent anticipation as the last of the women found a comfortable place to sit.

Performance

Indra leaned her forehead against the cool rock in the darkest recess of the deep shadow behind the main floor of the Sacred Cave. The time of the great storm flashed into her mind. She felt as if she were leaning, not against cool damp rock but against the dripping flank of her lover, the Great Whale. So vast and desolate was her sense of loss that a sob escaped her lips. She sank to the floor of the cave in a paroxysm of tears. This moment of deep mourning was as complete a healing as she had ever known. All the tension of the last few days of creative rehearsal fell away from her.

Members of the cast were standing facing the small entrance through which they would enter the Sacred Cave from behind the chimney rock. A young woman called Plaree, who was a mime artist, had sat down close to Indra. She looked uncertainly at Indra's prone form. It was usual for raft women to comfort each other. Plaree had been the first one to hear Indra sobbing at the back of the cave and she had run to her and knelt down beside her, but she had not, as was the custom, taken Indra in her arms to comfort her. Indra was no longer one of them — she seemed set apart, distanced by her off-raft experiences. There was a strangeness about her as if she had taken a step beyond their world into a place beyond their understanding. On a physical level the halo of white hair that framed her comparatively young face, gave Indra a strangely wild appearance, but this was not the greatest thing that distanced her from the familiar society of raft women.

Quite simply Indra had, during her strange, wanderings, acquired an aura, a beautiful glow that emanated from within her, although she did not know that it was apparent. Her being was radiant.

All this meant that, although Plaree wanted to comfort Indra, she held back in awe of this woman who had devised the great performance that was about to be enacted. After a while Indra sat up and looked at Plaree and smiled, holding out her arms to the younger woman. For a few moments they hugged.

'I am healed. Thank you for sitting with me,' whispered Indra, wiping away her tears. She stood up — the musicians, who were the nearest group to the entrance to the Sacred Cave, were looking around for Indra.

Mione, taller than many of the other women, looked at Indra over the heads of the others.

'They are all waiting, Indra,' she whispered loudly.

'Begin.' Indra whispered back, signalling with both arms that they should go forward from the comparative darkness of the deep shadows into the beautiful subtle light of the Sacred Cave.

Alaly, the composer of the overture, stepped into the middle of the floor of the Sacred Cave. She turned slowly. A moments stillness, then gently swaying she started to dance-conduct the musicians as they entered — each musician danced with her instrument as she played the subtle rhythms. When the final strands of the overture died away, the audience opened their arms wide, palms upturned and a low appreciative hum of excitement echoed around the Sacred Cave.

Indra lay back and was hoisted shoulder high by the nine women who represented the waves. They carried her to the entrance, waiting a moment for the musicians to clear to one side of the floor, where they would continue playing and swaying to the music. Indra held her body rigid in order that the dancers could lift her right above their heads as they entered the Sacred Cave. Indra felt a surge of excitement as they lifted her high into the air, her head dropped back and her long white hair cascaded down the arms of the two women who were supporting her shoulders on their upturned palms. It was never like this when I lay on my raft that morning, she thought as she was gently swayed by the women dancers below her. Poetic licence, she thought with a slightly playful smile.

The music was almost as she had imagined it that morning before the northern sky turned dark. Mione was playing the slate bells, the music of sunlight. Each "wave" dancer wore her green silk shawls elaborately tied with a wide blue cummerbund. After dancing and swaying with Indra held high, her golden body lit by shimmering sand-lights, the dancers lowered her gently to the floor of the cave. Slowly the "white bird" dancers wheeled around Indra. The air became fragrant with the scent of the white powder they had used as make up, their white silk robes billowed out from their bodies as they described the great air patterns of the white sea birds they imitated.

Suddenly Indra sat up, looking intently northwards. Musicians were silenced, dancers who had previously been waves and birds became raft women again pointing northwards and looking alarmed, taking frightened backward steps.

The musicians played a jarring raucous cacophony expressing the fear and agitation of the raft women. Indra, holding her silk cloak high above her head, to represent the raft sail, ran around the stage floor of the cave and disappeared into the shadows. The other dancers, staring intently northwards, backed slowly into the dark recess.

When the last dancer had disappeared from view, Indra danced into the candle-lit circle in full ceremonial dress. She knelt down in the centre of the stage and slowly began to chant the ancient song of high places. Its haunting melody, known to every adult raft woman, held a mystery which increased in depth each time it was remembered.

The audience was spellbound. Never before had anyone attempted a solo performance of this chant: the range was too vast for one singer. Indra had always felt the presence of the solo motif within the chant and she knew that this innovation might be unacceptable to certain raft women, but she felt it was a perfect expression of her being. The communication a solo rendition of the chant afforded was vital to their understanding of her journey. When the last notes died away to echoing silence, Indra gazed up at the tiers of raft women and she knew that she had reached them. Many eyes held tears at the beauty of the moment and many hands reached towards her in silent appreciation.

After discarding her ceremonial robes, Indra lifted up a small sky wing sheet that had been hidden under her robes. With arms outstretched she seemed to 'fly' slowly and gracefully around the semicircle of oil lamps that marked the boundary of the cave floor. She the 'flew' far out to the edges of the cave. Finally returning, she reached the last lamp. She turned towards the centre of the stage in a gliding simulation of a wing turn.

With a sudden movement she seemed to swoop and dive. She hit the cave floor hard with the palms of her hands, breaking the fall, although to the audience it looked uncontrolled and painful. A gasp of fear rippled through the cave and there was another gasp of wonder as a flare was lit, high up on the dark rock chimney. A white, seven foot woman was revealed, towering above the scene. This illusion was created by a long silk hanging from her shoulders down the chimney rock.

The actress playing Aaron pointed upwards with a long white stick to the dark recesses of the ceiling. She did this so intently that many of the raft women followed her gaze into the shadows. Her eyes described Indra's fall from the sky and ended up looking at the prone figure of Indra herself in her simple white under-silk. The music was high, cold and mysterious and many raft women experienced a shiver, a raising of the hair on the back of the neck, as they took in the majesty of the tall figure with long white hair. It was a powerful and commanding image.

After a long moment of complete stillness 'Aaron' changed this image by throwing the long white front panel of the robe over her shoulder, so that impression of great height was lost, but not the power of the vision. With great economy of movement and with a subtle elegance 'Aaron' climbed down the rock to the stage floor. When she alighted she walked purposefully towards Indra's prone figure, cradling her head and ministering to her with the magical and mystical movements Indra had seen the real Aaron use.

The audience was entranced, aware that what they were viewing was something beyond their previous experience. The music playing was totally unknown to them, with a rhythmic quality that verged on the hypnotic.

This music was the nearest thing Indra could devise from her memory of the melting stone that Aaron put beside the fire. As she listened, Indra felt she had achieved an essence of the strangeness of the music she had heard and felt well pleased.

In a few moments 'Aaron' held her hand and Indra rose elegantly to her feet and together they danced. Indra had taught the actress-dancer the high energetic leaps that she had learned from Aaron and also the special dance techniques that had so excited Indra and had shown her a new understanding of dance.

Indra then began writhing on the floor in fear and disorientation. She tried unsteadily to stand and fell over. Giddily she crashed about and the raft women murmured with concern. 'Aaron' soothed her and helped her walk more normally.

Finally they prepared for a journey and both left the stage.

Moments later a dancer with grey robes walked around the semi-circle of oil lamps, billowing behind her was a silk chiffon cloak with the painted image of a whale. She wore a cap and her shoulders were padded — these being traditional symbols of an actress playing a male part. Indra re-entered and mimed swimming towards the "whale" and together they danced an intensely sensual duet in which the movement and the music were perfectly entwined. The audience was left in no doubt that they were lovers. The whale left Indra asleep, covered in the chiffon silk cloak with the whale motif. The musicians played The Music of the Sea, a familiar piece to all the raft women; it was relaxing and comforting after all the strange things they had seen.

The dancers, playing the Cloud Generation, gathered furtively around the stage in silence. Some were dressed in male costume. They mimed the unfurling of the great theatre raft sail. In unison they swayed from side to side imitating the rise and fall of the waves. Suddenly Indra's presence on board was discovered, a discovery which clearly angered the Cloud Generation and a dance of conflict ensued. Indra sat up looking around her in a confused way. She held her head feverishly and one of the dancers came forward with a medicine bag.

The musicians who had played discordantly throughout the conflict now began to beat quietly on their drums. The Cloud Generation looked about them in dismay — a storm was coming. Everyone busied themselves in readiness for the impending storm. With a crescendo of drumming, the storm hit — all the dancers were impelled first to one side of the stage and then the other. Some mimed being hit by falling debris and several were washed overboard beyond the lights, confusion reigned.

Indra, wrapped in the whale cloak, was rolling as helplessly as the rest. Suddenly the drumming stopped. Many of the dancers sank down in despair and some examined the wreckage. Indra walked to the edge of the stage and from the shadows the dancer in grey appeared. Indra unwrapped the cloak and draped it around the whale's shoulders and rested her head against the folds of the cloak. The Cloud Generation stood quite still, watching Indra and the whale holding a long rigging spar. Suddenly, with an angry yell, they all rushed towards Indra and the whale, both of whom dropped out of sight.

Everyone, except the whale dancer, cleared away. The whale dancer staggered over the oil lamps onto the stage, trailing a red ribbon. Bravely the whale danced round and round the stage, trailing more and more red ribbons which had been hidden in the folds of the costume. In the centre of the stage the dancer whirled round and round on the spot — the red ribbons flying around until, finally, the scarlet bonds wound close, encasing the body in a red ribboned bondage that fell to the floor of the stage.

Indra had held onto the whale cloak when she had disappeared in order that the full dramatic death of the whale could be properly effected.

Now she pulled herself painfully, on her stomach, onto the stage wrapped in the cloak. When she saw the whale she managed to get unsteadily to her feet. With genuine tears in her eyes she limped over to the dead whale and gently covered it with the whale cloak, the whale motif, clearly visible was made almost three dimensional by the body beneath it. Many of the audience, too, were overcome by the emotion of this poignant moment. Indra knelt beside the whale and then lay down.

The Cloud Generation entered and they stood still as if shocked by the sight of Indra and the whale. Then a dancer with a medical bag ran over to Indra. She beckoned the other dancers to her and they lifted Indra gently and carried her away. The dancers that remained danced around the whale in pairs.

The women playing male dancers, wore padded shoulders and close caps. Each danced with a raft woman. The musician drummed a heartbeat rhythm. The sexual connotations of the dance become quite obvious to the audience and it was also apparent that the "males" were actively choosing the females they wished to dance with. In raft woman society it was always the women who chose the males at feast times. It had been so since time immemorial. Women had always chosen the males and males were always flattered by a woman's attentions. To see the males in the dance taking the lead in the choosing of partners was shocking. Some women in the audience stood up, actually distressed by what they saw. But soon the dance changed from one nightmare to another. The dancers, one at a time, fell over writhing and rolling in obvious distress — the music became disjointed and discordant again.

Indra appeared and touched each dancer gently. Gradually they began to recover and they helped each other up and away. Indra waved goodbye to the last stragglers retreating into the darkness. She walked deliberately over to the whale. She pulled off the whale's cloak and threw it into the shadows. Out of the folds of her shawls she brought another chiffon silk cloak. The whale dancer stood up and Indra tied the new cloak around the dancer's shoulders, this cloak was painted the symbol of the dolphin.

The music of the sea was played again as Indra and the dolphin danced together through the wave dancers with their sea coloured silks. The dolphin dancer finally retreated to the shadows and Indra was left alone in the centre of the floor.

After several moments silence the music started and the whole cast appeared from behind the dark rock chimney, signalling the end of the entertainment as Indra retreated into the shadows.

The musicians came forward, together with their conductor, bowed low and retreated. Indra returned as the cast and musicians drifted away to the edges and Indra was left facing her audience. Then she too, after bowing low, left the stage.

A heavy silence descended on the cave. The audience just did not know how to react to such an extraordinary performance. The silence lengthened, then the whispering started which became a muted murmur of conversation — but no one moved.

A young girl who had sat in the front row during the performance stood up and ran onto the stage as she had seen the raft women audience do at feast time performances. It was the raft women's form of congratulation to the performers. Indra emerged from the shadows, a flower in her hand, as was the custom. She ran towards the young girl and swung her round, smiling. 'Did you enjoy it, little Sarba?' Indra asked.

'It was wonderful, Indra. But it wasn't like any of the feast time dancing. I know the stories of the feast dances — but your story was different.'

'It is very different!' laughed Indra.

By now many of the audience were joining them on stage. Performers and musicians all carried flowers to give to the children. There was a buzz of excited conversation.

'Are you going to tell us the story, Indra?' asked Surbia.

'Tomorrow, at sunset, I will tell you my story.' replied Indra.

Weaving

Golden bars of sunlight lit the Western sea through low grey clouds that were tinged with sunset pink. No-one had seen Indra during the day and it was rumoured that she had stayed on the Island overnight.

Many who heard this news rejected it — no-one ever stayed on the Island at night. But the rumour persisted. Must she not, it was argued, have stayed on the Island when her sky wing crashed, and what of the tall white person portrayed in her story?

Indra had hoped that the show would provoke a great deal of comment and speculation in order to prepare the raft women for the strange story she was about to unfold. She smiled to herself as she sat in the centre of the stage quietly weaving at a silk loom, thinking of her time with Aaron in the last few hours.

When the Sacred Cave had emptied the night before Indra had stayed, unable to join the other raft women, even the people she had been working closely with during the last few days were making their way across the beach to the raft city.

"I am not one of them," she had thought to herself as she stood uncertainly at the mouth of the Sacred Cave.

She turned with a sense of poignant anti-climax, to descend the roughhewn stones that were the main stairway into the cave and saw her giant friend crossing the floor of the cave towards her.

'Aaron!' cried Indra, running swiftly down towards the yeti woman. They met at the bottom of the steps and Indra stood on the last step and reached up to hug Aaron who, in turn, bent low to embrace her friend. After a long moment they looked at each other and smiled deeply into each other's eyes.

'Will you come with me to the final cave, Indra? I have prepared a meal for us. We can sleep there.'

'I would love to see that cave again. It is so good to see you Aaron, you seem to look taller!' laughed Indra.

Aaron smiled. 'I seem taller because we are in your world now. 'Everything here is your size. Come, you must be tired, Indra, after all your work. I have been watching you. Let me carry you to the cave.'

So saying, Aaron picked Indra up like a babe in arms and walked towards the rock chimney beside the place of change. Aaron climbed effortlessly, despite her burden, and finally they merged with the dark shadows close to the ceiling of the cave.

Seated in the phosphorescent splendour of the final cave the two women ate the delicious meal that Aaron had prepared. She told Indra that the dance drama had been a wonderfully exciting experience to watch. Even from her high shadowy vantage point she had seen much that had intrigued her.

'I know now why you were chosen, Indra. You have great skill and love of your craft. Your energy is beautiful. I particularly liked the way I was portrayed.'

'Oh, Aaron, do you really think it worked?'

'It was certainly very thought-provoking and I imagine that is what you intended it to be, in order to give them a taste of the truth to come. But, Indra, what happened to you after we parted? You have taken so long to return to the Island. Did your sickness get worse when you returned to the rafts? Having seen the dance I am intrigued to know.'

'Tomorrow at sunset I will tell my story to my people, yawned Indra dreamily. 'Then you, too, will know. And I think you can help me. Do you have your music stone? But now I am tired Aaron — I feel that I must sleep.'

'Sleep well, my friend,' whispered Aaron as she wrapped Indra gently into the soft silk folds of her cloak.

*   *   *

Sitting there in the centre of the stage, quietly weaving, Indra watched the first groups of women arrive. She felt deeply relaxed from the deep massage that Aaron had given her naked body when she awoke that morning.

Indra had chosen to wear long white silk shawls. The effect, with her halo of wild white hair in the dimly lit cave, was quite dazzling. She looked an ethereal creature from another world and several of the younger girls gasped when they saw her.

Gradually the cave filled whilst Indra continued at her loom, looking up every once in a while to assess the filling of the cave.

When everyone was seated, Indra began to weave and tell her tale. She left out nothing as she wove her silk, threading the shuttle to and fro.

Several hours passed as she wove a beautiful rainbow pattern onto the large loom. There were pauses in the telling of the story. Times that were filled with strange music that echoed through the cavern behind the chimney rock. The watching women were entranced.

*   *   *

Hours later, when the moon was high, the raft women silently made their way back to the raft city, moored in the lea of the Island. A slight wind was gusting as they crossed the sands and each was deep in thought at the strange things she had heard Indra impart.

Indra stood at the mouth of the Sacred Cave, watching the silent women cross the sands. Aaron came up behind her silently. Aware of Aaron's presence, Indra turned and buried her head in the folds of Aaron's voluminous cloak and wept.

A little while later Aaron again carried Indra into the final cave. Silently Aaron cradled the little raft woman whom she loved. A tear rolled down the great white cheek of the yeti woman and splashed into Indra's hair — but Indra did not wake.

Finale

At the sunset on the third evening the raft women embarked on the Island shore. They stood in groups on the undulating dunes in front of the Sacred Cave. Their mood was sombre and all day discussions and arguments had broken out all over the raft system. How could it be true that they had once lived on the Island with the males, as Indra had said? Had the Cloud Generation really killed a whale? New land! Could it really be true? Who was the tall woman in white? There was a general air of unease and some disbelief amongst the women.

For hundreds of years certain raft women had gone to the Island to provision, or hold an evening ritual but never, in their history, had the whole population, both young and old, set foot on the Island together, leaving the raft system entirely empty. Many felt a sense of foreboding as they looked back at the empty rafts.

When they were all assembled on the shore, the council of women led the way up the steep path to the Sacred Cave. They had expected to see Indra in the centre of the stage as she had been the evening before, but instead the Sacred Cave was empty except for a large two handled cup in the centre of the stage.

Leacia crossed the stage and peered into the deep shadows beside the great chimney of rock

A few minutes later she re-emerged looking puzzled. She went over to the women's council who were sitting together and whispered to them, gesticulating and shaking her head.

The murmuring of the assembled crowd died away into silence and Leacia looked up.

From the darkness above the chimney of rock, two white haired figures emerged. They stood for a while high above the upturned faces. The smaller of the two figures started to descend the rock chimney towards the floor of the cave. When she reached the ground Indra walked over to the ornate cup in the centre of the cave and sat beside it.

She looked up at her silent audience.

'Aaron the guardian of the mountain is here with us. I have decided that I would like her to be with us this evening.' Indra looked over towards where the women's council were sitting in full ceremonial dress. 'May she come down and join us?'

The women's council bent their heads together and conferred for a few minutes but their curiosity overcame their reservation and Leacia spoke. 'The mountain woman is welcome among us.'

Everyone, except Indra, watched with fascination as the yeti woman descended with lithe agility, into the light of the cave. Until yesterday they had not known of her existence on the Island. Even today many had been somewhat sceptical as to this aspect of Indra's story. Although the raft generations who provisioned on the Island never ventured, even on sky wings, more than a few miles into the Island's interior, they found it hard to believe there had been an unknown presence on the great white mountain.

On reaching the floor of the cave, Aaron stepped forward towards the earthenware cup that was so large it could only be lifted by the two handles by Aaron herself.

There was an intake of breath from the raft women as Aaron's white being emerged from the shadows into the light. She was a magnificent commanding figure and, as she neared, the raft women got to their feet, as if hypnotised, in an appreciation of her great presence.

'I greet you, raft women,' she intoned in her resonant multi-faceted voice. 'Please, let us sit down.' Aaron stood on the other side of the great cup. She looked over and smiled at Indra as the women sat down in complete silence, waiting, fascinated to hear again the beautiful tones of Aaron's orchestral voice.

'All that Indra told you yesterday evening is true. Your ancestors did live on this Island — both males and women together in one large settlement.'

The raft women murmured to each other, still mystified at such a revelation.

'It is taboo for you to live on the Island only because my ancestor, Sumi, made it so. You originally lived as one society that became divided and exiled because it was the only way to save the Island which sustains your existence. The males had almost destroyed the island so they could not be allowed to return. Before Indra wove her story yesterday, you had no knowledge of how your raft system came to be. Sumi my ancestor reached deep into the minds of your gathered ancestors and so for the males it became taboo for them to set foot on the island.

'This Island is now no longer alone. In the vastness of the ocean a new land has been formed and whether you welcome it or not, the Great Spirit has changed your world.

I believed, originally, that Indra had been sent to me to be a messenger — to tell you of your history and so to free you. But there was more for her to understand. Another great journey to be undertaken.

The Great Whale knew of the new land for which Indra searched, and as whales are pure love he communicated his great love to her. It was for her creativity and love, he chose her.'

A long sigh went up from the raft women at the end of this hypnotically beautiful vocal symphony. Aaron looked round at the assembled company with her large, ice-blue eyes.

'The Great Spirit took Indra on a further journey, to the shores of the new land itself, as she has told you. She has entertained you and she has woven her story. Now she must speak to you of what is in her heart.'

Indra looked into Aaron's limpid eyes and stood up. Then she looked at the tiers of raft women seated on the rocks of the Sacred Cave.

For a moment or two she was unable to speak. To perform for them and to tell her story had not been easy but, now that she had to be herself, she found this to be the hardest challenge of all. Indra took a large breath and said softly, 'Aaron says that I must speak from the heart and it is true that I must. The Cloud Generation have done terrible things and I have felt anger towards them.'

When the echoes died away she resumed a quieter voice, 'But I have known great love and I have known great change and these are the two themes that I must communicate to you. If, at the time of returning, we drink this cup together, I will know that I have succeeded in what I set out to do.'

'You all know well that there are some very good reasons why I should not care about the fate of the Cloud Generation. They took our theatre raft — so dear to my heart — and it is now virtually destroyed, beyond repair, so they are stranded on the new land. You also know how the males behaved towards the young women and how the young women also drank the fermented drink. They killed the Great Whale and at the height of the storm I believe in a moment of madness that they almost killed me.'

Indra let the shocked murmuring between the women settle into silence. Raft women only gathered fish that were gifted onto the raft system, they never killed.

'My love for the Great Whale transcends death and within that great love I care about the fate of the Cloud Generation because their fate is our fate.'

Indra paused a moment to let the impact of her last statement set in.

'What happens to them will ultimately happen to us. If they flourish and make the new land theirs, then our civilisation will survive this change and continue for untold generations living on both lands.'

Indra again paused for the echoing exclamations to cease. It had not occurred to them that land could be lived on, they had lived for so many generations on their rafts.

'If we leave the Cloud Generation there without support they might manage to survive and may become hostile, or they will cease to exist and we will continue unchanged into oblivion. Fewer and fewer of our males may return to us at feast time, preferring to live on the new land that they have sought for so long, rather than be provisioned by us. Our young people will grow restless to see the new land and be part of something exciting, and they will begin to leave us.'

'We have to embrace this new land and these young people who broke all the rules. At this time of great change they have led the way. I believe that the Great Spirit formed the new land and intended us to change and grow, and that the Cloud Generation felt the impact of the change and were carried along by it. They need provisions urgently!'

Some mothers of the Cloud Generation exclaimed and looked concerned by this new urgency.

'The males that have arrived here can navigate our raft city northwards to the shores of the new land. It will mean going out of sight of the Island, but the Cloud Generation's lives are in the balance and so is our future. We must provision our rafts and bring them supplies.'

'I believe it is the Great Spirit's will that we should know the true meaning love, which means we must also know the pain it may bring, as well as its joy. We must help the Cloud generation despite their actions.'

Aaron lifted her large two-handled vessel. 'The cup is here if you wish to drink from it. It will signal your consent'

Every eye turned to the magnificent mountain woman that had exhorted them to drink from the great cup that she held towards them. Her symphonic multi-faceted voice held a compelling fascination.

After a moment's hesitation, Leacia, the most respected woman in the council, stepped forward onto the floor of the cave. Aaron offered her the loving cup.

Indra came forward to greet Leacia and brought her to the centre of the Sacred Cave. Leacia looked up into Aaron's eyes for a long moment, then she and Aaron both held the cup whilst she drank.

*   *   *

The two white haired women stood on the windswept ridge, close to the mouth of Aaron's cave. Together they watched, from their high vantage point, the great exodus — the laden flotilla of multi-coloured sails that had never before sailed together. The women and the males were combined in a common purpose, sailing northwards from the Island in the pearl grey morning light.

'Some will return.' said Aaron.

'It is the rolling of the stone,' replied Indra in a voice full of hope tinged with sadness. 'Our time is one of great motion and change.'

A tear rolled down her cheek. She let it drop into the palm of her hand.

'Goodbye, Mione.' she called.

Dear Reader
If you have enjoyed reading this book, then
please leave a review on Amazon.
Thank you.

11631256R00113

Printed in Great Britain
by Amazon.co.uk, Ltd.,
Marston Gate.